W9-CID-433

For those who remember . . .

THE TWILIGHT ZONE

was a television series that ran originally on CBS from 1959 to 1964. Close to eight million people accepted the invitation of its master of ceremonies, Rod Serling, to travel beyond the realm of reality into this rarefied Zone where the improbable sprang into being before their eyes and challenged them to new understanding. "The Twilight Zone" was a cultural phenomenon, entertainment with both magic and message. In syndication, the show has reached millions more with the same impact.

For those who have never seen
THE TWILIGHT ZONE

a new world is about to be opened where the suspension of disbelief leads through bizarre experience into basic truth. As an act of homage four film directors, Steven Spielberg, Joe Dante, George Miller, and John Landis, brought you the Warner Bros. movie. Now Robert Bloch translates its dramatic impact into print for you.

Introductions quoted on the back cover are by Rod Serling for the TV series.

Books by
ROBERT BLOCH

Psycho
Psycho II
Twilight Zone: The Movie

Published by
WARNER BOOKS

TWILIGHT ZONE
THE MOVIE

a novel by

ROBERT BLOCH

Segment 1: *Written by* JOHN LANDIS

Segment 2: *Story by* GEORGE CLAYTON JOHNSON
Screenplay by GEORGE CLAYTON JOHNSON *and* RICHARD MATHESON *and* JOSH ROGAN

Segment 3: *Screenplay by* RICHARD MATHESON
Based on a story by JEROME BIXBY

Segment 4: *Screenplay by* RICHARD MATHESON
Based on a story by RICHARD MATHESON

"TWILIGHT ZONE -THE MOVIE"
DAN AYKROYD · ALBERT BROOKS · SCATMAN CROTHERS · JOHN LITHGOW · VIC MORROW · KATHLEEN QUINLAN
Produced by STEVEN SPIELBERG and JOHN LANDIS Music by JERRY GOLDSMITH Executive Producer FRANK MARSHALL
Story by GEORGE CLAYTON JOHNSON

Screenplay by GEORGE CLAYTON JOHNSON and   Based on a story by JEROME BIXBY   Based on a story by RICHARD MATHESON
Written by JOHN LANDIS   RICHARD MATHESON and JOSH ROGAN   Screenplay by RICHARD MATHESON   Screenplay by RICHARD MATHESON
Directed by JOHN LANDIS   Directed by STEVEN SPIELBERG   Directed by JOE DANTE   Directed by GEORGE MILLER

DOLBY STEREO   READ THE WARNER   SOUNDTRACK AVAILABLE ON   A FILM WARNER BROS
IN SELECTED THEATRES   PAPERBACK   WARNER BROS. RECORDS   A WARNER COMMUNICATIONS COMPANY

WARNER BOOKS

A Warner Communications Company

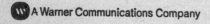

TWILIGHT ZONE
THE MOVIE

1

BILL

Bill Conner fought his way through the early-evening traffic with more than his usual quota of curses as he maneuvered the Ford into the right-hand lane and prepared to make his turn.

Sure as hell, just as he slid into position, the light changed!

Story of my life, he told himself. Every time I

think I'm getting someplace, there it goes again
—they stop me cold.

His fingers drummed impatiently against the
steering wheel as he scowled into the headlight glare
of the bumper-to-bumper traffic reflected in his
rearview mirror. Even before the signal turned green
again, his foot hit the gas pedal and he started to
swing around the corner.

Through the windshield, his eyes caught a blur of
movement, and the sound of a sudden shout mingled
with the squeal of brakes as his car halted, barely
missing the stream of pedestrians directly in its path
along the crosswalk.

Bill leaned out of the window to get a better
glimpse of their frightened faces as they scurried by.

Black faces, of course. Whole damned neighborhood was full of them.

"Why the hell don't you watch where you're
going?" he shouted.

The crosswalk cleared and he completed his turn,
sliding into the comparative safety of the side street.

With an effort he forced himself to relax his
pressure on the gas pedal. Better slow down, try to
take it easy. The last thing he needed now was an
accident. Some damned hopped-up jig steps in front
of your car and the next thing you know there's a Jew
lawyer coming at you with a million-dollar damage
suit.

Bill leaned forward and switched on the radio. A
little music to soothe his nerves, that's what he
needed. *Just a song at twilight*—

A blast of raucous sound assailed his ears and a

high-pitched female voice screamed in insane invitation.

"Give it to me, baby—"

Bill cut off the voice, wishing that he could cut her throat instead. Goddam jungle bunnies! Bad enough they'd taken over the streets—now they'd taken over the air, too. Getting so they didn't even leave a white man room enough to take a decent breath anymore.

What the hell was happening to this country anyway? Things were different when he was a kid. You didn't hear all this crap about civil rights; those people did their jobs and kept their places. Now the whole damned world was turning into one big welfare state, nothing but taxes and more taxes, and for what? Nobody had the guts to stop it, nobody even dared to speak out against it anymore. All this drinking and doping, all these newspaper stories about robberies and rapings, muggings and murders, crime in the streets—crazy, that's what it was. Just crazy.

Too bad they didn't have someone like himself running things; he could clean up the whole mess in a hurry. Take the crime situation, for example —first thing to do is kill off eighty percent of the lawyers, ninety percent of the psychiatrists, and a hundred percent of the kind of people who started off a sentence with "Hey, man."

Bill shook his head. No sense letting himself go overboard. The way things were going, decent hardworking citizens like himself didn't stand a prayer. All he could hope for was a little rest and relaxation, something to take his mind off his troubles—particularly after a day like the one he'd just had. At least they couldn't take that away from him—not yet, anyway.

The bright lights of a bar flashed ahead on his left. Bill slowed the car, seeking a parking spot alongside the right-hand curb. He finally found one, half a block ahead. Cutting his headlights and turning off the engine, he stepped out into the street, making sure that he'd locked the door behind him. The old neighborhood wasn't safe anymore; leave your car unlocked for a minute and kiss it good-bye forever. That's progress for you. Once upon a time all they stole was chickens and watermelons; now, if you didn't keep your eyes open, they'd take your car or your wallet—even your life.

Bill shrugged, shaking off the thought, then squared his shoulders as he crossed the street and moved in the direction of the entrance beneath the neon light. It was Happy Hour time. No sense walking in with a frown on his face. *Remember, you're a salesman, and the first job of a good salesman is to sell himself.*

The place was crowded with customers, homeward-bound like he was, who'd stopped off en route to unwind for a moment after a long hard day.

Bill turned and scanned the far edges of the crowd, then caught sight of the familiar figures seated in the far corner booth.

The two men were almost mirror images of himself; Ray was perhaps a few years older and

Larry a trifle younger, but both wore similar outfits—double-knit suits, white shirts, the kind of conservative necktie calculated to inspire confidence in a potential customer. Two good salesmen, two good buddies.

Now they looked up at him and returned his wave of greeting. Ray moved around to the center of the booth as Bill slid into the seat behind him.

"What took you so long?" he said.

"Goddam heavy traffic. Getting so a guy could make better time walking." Bill glanced down at his watch. "Hey, look, you guys—I can only stay a couple of minutes. The old lady's got some cousins from Florida coming over for dinner."

Larry eyed him across the table. "Then, you better hurry and catch up." He turned and signaled to a scantily clad waitress as she passed the booth. "Hey, girl! Another beer over here. Better make it two."

Obviously, Larry was feeling no pain. Ray seemed to be the more sober of the two; as Bill spoke, he was conscious of Ray's stare.

"Something biting you?" Ray asked. "What's wrong?"

"The whole goddam world, that's what's wrong."

Across the table Larry met his scowling gaze with a grimace of mock dismay. "Oh-oh!"

Ignoring him, Bill turned to Ray. "Remember that guy Goldman?"

"So that's it. You didn't get promoted." Ray nodded. "What happened?"

"They passed me up for the Jew bastard."

The waitress set two glasses of beer on the tabletop in front of Bill and he turned, his scowl vanishing at the sight of her cleavage as she bent forward. Reaching out, he made a grab for her rounded buttocks. "How'd you like to cheer up an old man?" he murmured.

The waitress pulled away with a deftness born of long practice. "Just drink your beer and you'll feel better."

Bill grabbed her again. "Come on, honey—"

The waitress jerked free of his grasp, eyes blazing. *"Take your hands off me, buster!"*

As she flounced off, Larry started to laugh. "I think she likes you, Bill. You sure got a way with the women."

Ray didn't share his mirth. "Too bad about the job," he said.

Bill's scowl returned. *"I'm better than Goldman. I've been there seventeen years, for Christ's sake!"*

Larry fumbled for his glass and raised it tipsily. "Come on, Bill, relax!"

"Relax, hell! Goldman takes my promotion and I should relax? That's six grand a year more than I'm earning now."

Ray shook his head. "Easy, Bill—"

"Easy for him, you mean. The Jews always get more money."

"How long has Goldman been there?" Ray asked quietly.

Bill shrugged. "So he's been there longer than me! What of it? I've sold more units in the last six

14

weeks than that kike has moved all year." As he spoke, he felt the anger rising within him, spilling out. "You know me. I'm a hard worker. I work my butt off and some smart Jewboy gets my job! Bunch of smart operators—no wonder they own everything!"

"Come off it, Bill." Ray leaned forward. "You know better than that. The Jews do not own everything."

"That's right," Larry chuckled, nodding. "The A-rabs won't let 'em!"

"Never mind that," Bill muttered. "Arabs are just niggers wrapped in sheets."

Ray glanced at Larry and sighed in weary resignation. "Oh, no—he's on a roll now!"

Larry snickered, but Bill ignored the reaction. "Life in this country is getting harder and harder." He thumped his fist down on the tabletop. "And you know why? It's the Jews and the blacks and gooks, that's why."

"You're raving, Bill." There was a note of caution in Ray's reply, a note that Bill ignored as his own voice rose loudly.

"Raving? My house is owned by some gook bank! I've got niggers living just six blocks from my home."

He broke off abruptly at the sound of another voice rising from behind him.

"Excuse me, mister. You got a problem?"

Bill glanced up into the face of a tall man standing beside the booth. The face was black.

15

Across the table, Larry muttered under his breath. "Oh-oh!"

Bill stared up defiantly. "Yeah, I do, buddy. I got a lot of problems."

The black face was impassive. "Look," he said slowly, "I really don't care what you gentlemen think, as long as we don't have to listen to it."

Before Bill could reply, Ray broke in quickly. "It's okay, no sweat. Our friend's a little upset. That's all."

Out of the corner of his eye, Bill caught his warning glance and forced himself to turn, nodding toward the formidable figure standing beside him. "Sure, sure," he said. "Everything's under control."

For a moment the black patron hesitated, his eyes fixed on Bill's face. Then he turned and moved back to his table. Bill reached for one of the glasses in front of him and downed its contents at a single gulp.

As he reached for the other glass, Ray frowned. "Maybe we ought to cut out," he said.

Bill shook his head. "You do what you damn well please! I'm not gonna leave until I'm good and ready. If that nigger doesn't like what I got to say, let *him* get out."

"Keep your voice down!" Ray set an example with his worried whisper. "You want to get us killed?"

An inner censor modulated the sound of Bill's voice but not the message it conveyed. "Hitler had the right idea. You just kill all of them."

He raised his glass and drank as Larry nodded in alcoholic agreement. "That's where we screwed up, in Vietnam, right there."

"What?" Ray blinked as Larry nodded again.

"If we just killed them all off, we would've won."

Ray's gesture mingled disgust with dismissal. "You're drunk, Larry."

Larry ignored the observation, waggling a forefinger to emphasize his words of wisdom. "You see, if they were dead, then they wouldn't be Communists."

"Oh no? Why couldn't someone be a dead Communist?"

"Hey, I never thought of that! Those Communists sure are tricky bastards."

His loud laughter was infectious; Ray's chuckle responded, but Bill sat stony-faced, immune to the contagion.

Larry glanced at him, concerned. "Come on, Bill. Lighten up!"

Bill downed the contents of his second glass, then banged it down on the table. "You think this is funny?" he said. "Some friends you are! That Jew gets my job, some nigger threatens me when I speak up, and all you can do is laugh about it. I'm sure one hell of a lucky guy to have friends like you."

Ray reached out and put his hand on Bill's shoulder. "Let's split," he said. "You're getting loud again."

Bill pushed his arm away and rose. He was ready

17

to leave, but not before he made his point. "Just remember one thing. While you two guys were screwing up, I was in the war. We were paid to kill gooks."

"Hey," Ray said. "Just cool it—"

Bill wasn't listening. "I thought we won that war but now those same gooks own my house! And then this Jew comes along and grabs my promotion. I could use that extra money. I was counting on it. Instead I get myself shafted by some rich Jew—"

"Now wait a minute." Ray shook his head reprovingly. "I know Goldman and you can't exactly call him rich. Judging by the kind of clothes he wears and that old car of his, you're probably in better financial shape than he is."

"What the hell difference does that make?" Bill made no effort to control his voice now; as far as he was concerned everybody could get the message, loud and clear. "Don't you understand? I'm better than a Jew. I'm better than an African. I'm better than an Oriental. I'm an American, dammit! That's supposed to mean something!"

Turning, he started along the row of booths, heading for the door.

Ray's voice rose behind him. "Bill— Wait a minute—"

But there was no time to wait. Yanking the door open, he strode out into the twilit street. Somewhere behind him the door banged shut.

Bill didn't hear it. He was too busy staring; staring into the street before him, where everything was—

Wrong.

The traffic had vanished. So had half the parked cars lining the curb opposite him. And those that remained were—different. Something about their sizes and shapes reminded him vaguely of the old jalopies he'd used when he was a kid; that's what they looked like, but even so he couldn't recognize the models. Behind them, a row of storefronts remained, but even these looked strange and unfamiliar. All of the fronts were dark, closed for the night. Directly across the way was a shop with a broken display window; half of the glass had been shattered and knocked out of its frame. Across the wooden door were two words, their letters scrawled in splotches of yellow paint.

Bill squinted through the dusk, trying to make them out.

Juden, and *Juif.*

One word was German and the other French, but both had the same meaning—Jews.

And what the hell had happened here? Glancing around, he noticed other changes—banners dangling from poles before the shops, each emblazoned with a design that also reminded him of something seen in the distant past: a squiggle of angling interlocking black lines forming the shape of a swastika.

What gives here? Blinking, Bill turned away to confront a brick wall beside the bar entrance. It was plastered with posters bearing boldfaced lettering in German and French. Once again Bill realized, startled, that he could read and understand the wording.

He shook his head, trying to clear it. Was he

drunk? No way—not on just two beers. And even if he'd had a dozen, that still wouldn't explain why he was able to understand foreign languages. And it wouldn't explain why he didn't recognize this street.

What had happened to it? And what had happened to *him?*

Bill closed his eyes for a moment, shutting out the strangeness. He was uptight, that was it. He shouldn't have let himself get carried away like that back there in the bar. All he had to do now was to get control of himself again. He stood quietly, taking deep breaths, forcing in fresh air to clear his lungs and his head. That should do the trick.

But when he opened his eyes again, nothing had changed.

Nothing—and everything. He was still standing on a strange street, staring at the strange store-fronts, the ancient, unfamiliar automobiles, the peculiar posters with their foreign lettering.

Now as he glanced up, he saw a moving vehicle rounding the corner at his left. It too was of ancient vintage, and its side door bore the emblem of a swastika against a circular background. The car screeched to a halt at the curb before him. The rear door swung open and two men emerged quickly. Both were wearing uniforms—uniforms that Bill had seen many times before, but only in old news-photos and movies of World War Two.

Bill stared at them as they approached, stunned by the sudden shock of recognition. *Jesus Christ—these guys were Nazi officers!*

"Ou allez-vous?" The first man's eyes were cold, his voice curt. "Who are you?"

"Qui êtes-vous?" Bill turned to face the second officer as he extended his hand.

"Ihre Papirn."

Bill stood silent, suddenly realizing that both officers were addressing him in a foreign tongue; the first in French and the second in German, and yet he understood what they were saying. How could that be?

The first officer was speaking again. Once more the language was French, but Bill understood the words of command all too clearly. "Your papers! Now!"

Bill started to back away. *"Vos papiers! Maintenant."*

The first officer grabbed his arm, then reached into Bill's coat pocket for his wallet.

Bill shook his head. "Hey, what the hell do you think you're doing—"

The second officer slapped his face. *"Sei still!"* he shouted.

The stinging blow brought tears to Bill's eyes, and before he could speak again, the first officer had grabbed his wallet; now he was rifling its plastic pockets and examining their contents. He peered down at Bill's Master Charge card.

"Qu'est-ce que c'est que ça?" he snapped.

Bill frowned in bewilderment, then recoiled as the second man slapped his face again.

"Antwortensie!" the Nazi shouted. *"Was meint das?"*

Bill forced his voice. "It's a credit card for Christ's sake!"

"Sind Sie Englischer?" the second officer demanded. *"Was tun Sie hier?"*

Bill groped for an answer. What *was* he doing here? And just where was he? He stared past his two interrogators, stared at the signs identifying the storefront across the street. The signs were in French, but these men were German. Vaguely he remembered his history lessons when he was still a kid in school. The Nazis had occupied France during World War Two. But that was in 1940, a lifetime ago. How could they be here now?

The first officer held up Bill's driver's license. *"Vous êtes Américain? Répondez-moi!"*

"What are you doing here?" the second officer repeated. Stepping behind Bill, he grabbed his arms, holding him fast.

"Let go of me!" Bill shouted.

The first officer shook his head. *"Venez avec nous!"* He closed the wallet and stuffed it into his pocket, then turned and started across the walk to the waiting car. His companion began to propel Bill forward. As they reached the open car door, Bill yanked himself free and turned quickly, lunging at his captor and pushing him back against the other officer.

The two men collided forcefully, and for a moment they stumbled off-balance. Bill turned and ran down the street.

Shouts rose behind him: *"Halt!"* *"Arrêtez!"*

Bill did not look back. He ran forward blindly with a speed born of panic.

Again the shouts sounded: *"Halt! Ich werde schie Ben!"*

Bill opened his eyes just in time to see the entrance to an alleyway yawning to his left. As he swerved into it, he heard the echo of two shots from behind. He raced up the alley, weaving his way amidst a litter of garbage and broken pieces of furniture. In the darkness he stumbled and fell.

For a moment he lay there, trying to catch his breath. Panting, he raised his head and glanced back just in time to see his pursuers appear at the end of the alleyway behind him. Both men were holding pistols now, and as their eyes scanned the darkness they raised the weapons, firing blindly.

Pain lanced Bill's left arm just below the shoulder. He glanced down, shocked at the sight of the bleeding wound. From the darkness beyond came the sound of running feet pounding against the cobblestones.

Glancing around frantically, Bill saw a pile of rubble projecting from the wall directly beside him. Soundlessly, he slid behind it and crouched down, breathing a silent prayer that his hiding place was secure.

Afraid to lift his head, he could only lie silently as the sound and tempo of running feet increased, then diminished in darkness beyond. Only then did he dare to lift his head and peer forward to the other end of the alley. In the light from the street beyond, he saw that the officers had halted, glancing about in confusion.

For a moment Bill felt safe—but only for a

moment. Now the air resounded with a shrill shriek of a whistle, summoning aid.

Bill's throbbing arm was warm with blood, his forehead cold with sweat. Peering out from behind the rubble, he saw a wooden door set in the brick wall of the alley directly across from him. Gasping, he rose and dashed toward it. He tugged at the door handle, hoping against hope that he'd find it unlocked. To his relief, the door gave way, opening inward.

He entered, closing the door behind him. Slowly his eyes penetrated the gloom. Directly before him loomed a flight of stairs. He moved toward it quietly, then began to climb.

Halfway between the foot of the stairs and the landing above him he paused, startled by a sudden sound of footsteps overhead.

Again, the cold sweat broke out on his forehead. Someone was coming but there was no place to hide. He stood there, trapped.

Then footsteps faded and he heard the creak of a door opening and closing somewhere above.

Bill waited for a moment, giddy with the wave of pain that pulsed through his left arm. He strained to listen, but no further sound broke the silence.

Slowly he continued his climb. When he reached the landing above, he halted again, glancing from left to right along the small hallway. There were doors at either end. From behind the one at his right, he heard the faint and muffled murmur of conversation. Moving toward it, he could make out the source of the sound more clearly—a woman's voice, speaking French.

Bill couldn't tell what she was saying. The mere fact that she was French and female was enough of a relief to determine his decision.

Slowly, he pushed the door open and entered the room beyond.

He found himself standing in the confines of a shabby kitchen, illuminated by the light from a single bare bulb dangling on a cord above a table. Seated around it were three small children who now glanced up from their supper in surprise as he appeared. Standing before the wood stove at one side was a middle-aged woman, obviously their mother. Her dress was drab, her hair disheveled, her eyes widened in surprise.

Bill turned to her, his own eyes pleading. "Don't be afraid," he said. "I won't hurt you."

The mother made no reply. The children stared at him silently; then, in response to the woman's gesture they rose from their seats and moved toward her. The mother stepped before them as they huddled behind her for protection.

"Please—you've got to help me," Bill murmured. "I've been shot."

The woman gave him a puzzled glance, then her eyes darted toward the small window at the far corner of the room as the sound of sirens wailed up from the streets below.

Bill's voice rose, trying to drown them out. "I don't know what's happening to me. It's like I'm in a dream or something—"

The woman wasn't listening to him. But now as the screech of the sirens grew louder, her face firmed in sudden decision. In three quick steps she was at the window—raising it—leaning out—shouting down into the street below.

Her words were in French but Bill understood them all too clearly.

"Aidez-nous!" she screamed. *"Il est ici! Le Juif est ici!"*

Bill took a step forward. "Please—don't let them find me—"

His voice was lost in the sound of her screaming. *"Le Juif que vous cherchez est ici! En haut!"*

Bill turned and the children cowered, gazing up at him in fright, but their fear was nothing compared to his own as he heard the answering voices shouting up from the street below and the drumming of running feet against the pavement.

He lurched through the opened doorway to the landing beyond. Staring down, he saw the door burst open at the foot of the stairs. A uniformed man glanced up, meeting his startled gaze, then turned to call out to his companion. His language was German.

"Das ist er."

A rush of footsteps and a babble of voices rose in answer. As soldiers began pouring through the doorway of the landing below, Bill turned and raced back into the kitchen.

Slamming the door, he barred it from the inside. Behind him the woman screamed again and the children started to cry. Bill ignored them, moving to the window and staring out at the drop below. The street was temporarily deserted but he couldn't chance jumping—at this height the fall could be fatal.

Now the room resounded with frantic echoes as the soldiers began pounding on the door.

There was a sudden crash as one of the upper panels splintered under the impact of a rifle butt.

Bill reached out with his good arm, finding and grasping the cornice above the window. Firming his grip, he swung out and pulled himself upward, his feet braced against the side of the window frame.

Exerting all his strength, he clung to the projection with both hands, not daring to look down at the street below. For a moment he hung swaying, his feet moving pendulum-like in empty air; then he raised himself over the cornice and onto the rooftop. Now a faint babble arose from the street, but Bill didn't look down. Panting for breath, he rose and ran across the roof, continuing his route across the roof of the building beyond it.

From behind and below, a voice shouted in German. *"Er ist am Dach! Ich will schnell eine Licht."*

Glancing down, Bill saw a soldier climbing out of the window of the room he had just vacated.

Dizzy with exertion, he turned and stared across the alley where another rooftop rose. This one was slanted and tiled. Bill glanced at it dubiously but the sound of voices from below firmed his resolution. In a minute they'd be up here and he had no choice, nowhere else to go.

Breathing deeply, he moved to the edge of the roof, forcing himself to look down just long enough to estimate the distance between this building and the next.

Eight feet—maybe nine. He could make it. Hell, what was he talking about? He *had* to make it!

He stepped back, taking another deep breath, then ran forward and leaped from the parapet, landing on the slanted surface opposite with a thump that squeezed the air from his lungs. His fingers found a purchase on the tiles, but even when he exerted all his strength, he was unable to pull himself upward. The darkness had deceived him; the angle of the roof was too steep for him to climb with nothing but tiles to cling to.

Suddenly a beam of light flared across the surface of the roof directly beside him.

Bill glanced down over his left shoulder for a glimpse of the alleyway below. His eyes watered as he stared into the blinding ray of an upturned searchlight resting in the back of an open jeep. As the light swept on, its path was followed by a hail of rifle shots. The soldiers were firing up, guided by the beam.

Frantically, Bill made another effort to edge his way up along the steep slant of the rooftop, favoring his right hand.

There was a sudden splintering sound and Bill glanced up along his arm to its source: the tile he clung to had cracked and broken loose.

"Oh no!" he gasped.

Scrabbling, his fingers clawed nothing but empty

air, and he felt himself starting to slide back toward the edge of the roof behind him. And now the beam of the searchlight swooped, then halted directly upon him, pinning him in its harsh glare.

Bill closed his eyes. In a moment now, the shots would come.

Suddenly, from below, a voice sounded in command. *"Halt Feurer!"*

There were no shots, and no need for them, because they could see what was happening. They could see him sliding down the slant toward the edge of the roof.

Bill clawed out again, gripping another tile to halt his descent, then groaned in dismay as he felt it tear loose from beneath his frantic fingers.

A sudden blast of cold air welled up from below and he realized to his horror that his legs were now dangling over the edge.

Then he began to slide faster.

"Please, God!" he whispered. "Please help me—"

Tiles scraped against his body and tore at the side of his cheek as he slipped backward. As he went over the edge, his right arm rose to grab the drainage gutter; now his fingers closed around it and for a moment he hung swaying over the alleyway below.

Then he fell.

Bill hit the ground with an impact that drove the breath from his body.

Ground. He was lying on the ground.

And that meant he was still alive, still conscious.

It was a miracle, that's what it was—a goddam miracle. That rooftop was at least three stories above the cobblestones of the alleyway.

Cobblestones—

Bill was lying facedown, his left cheek pressed against the ground. And it *was* ground; not cold, hard stone, but soft, warm grass.

Something was wrong here—very wrong.

Bill started to open his eyes, but before he could do so, hands gripped his shoulders roughly, turning him over and slamming him down on his back.

Now his eyes were open. He stared up into the night sky, into the circle of figures gazing down at him. "No!" he cried.

He was lying on his back in a forest clearing. Flames flickered under the hanging branches of the trees—flames of torches held in the hands of white-robed, hooded figures standing over him.

A shock of recognition surged through him.

White robes—armed men squinting down at him through eyeholes in their hoods. The Ku Klux Klan!

"No!" Bill cried again.

One of the hooded figures laughed. "We got you now, nigger!"

Nigger? What was he talking about?

Bill opened his mouth, but before he could speak, two of the Klansmen grabbed him by the shoulder and pulled him to his feet.

Then he found his voice. "Where am I?"

A hooded man cradling a rifle shook his head. "Shut up!" Turning, he nodded to the man standing at his right. "Tie his hands," he said.

The hooded figure nodded, then stepped behind Bill to join his companions as they jerked their captive's wrists out behind his back and pinned them together. Bill felt the rough rope looping around his wrists.

He looked up, shaking his head. "What's the idea? Why are you doing this to me?"

The Klansman before him raised his rifle in a menacing gesture. "Shut up, nigger!"

Bill stared at him, frowning. "What are you talking about? I'm a white man!"

Hands gripped his shoulders from behind, pitching him forward. He fell facedown upon the grassy knoll, and landed hard, unable to break his fall because his wrists were now firmly tied together behind his back.

The Klansman with the rifle moved toward him, and Bill felt a jab of pain as a booted foot emerged from beneath the hem of the white robe, kicking him over on his back again.

"You hear me, boy? I said for you to shut up!"

Bill gaped upward, swallowing hard, hoping against hope as he made one last attempt. "I'm white! Can't you see? Look at me—"

The Klansman with the rifle leaned forward, a mirthless chuckle sounding from behind his hanging hood.

He swung his rifle barrel down, smashing it into Bill's stomach. "Don't talk back to me, boy! We gonna learn you some respect."

Bill lay silent, fighting the pain, and the nausea welling up behind it.

A low murmur sounded from the half-circle of hooded figures behind him. From their midst one voice rose clearly. "Let's hang the son of a bitch!"

Clutching hands reached down, yanking Bill to his feet. Holding him tightly, they jerked him around to face the moss-festooned boughs of a huge tree. Something flamed and flared beside it, a burning cross, six feet high, the base wedged into the ground. By its light and by the light of the torches carried by the Klansmen, Bill could see hooded shadows reflected against the treetops of the forest surrounding the clearing.

Hoods . . . torches . . . cross-burning . . . they *had* to be insane! Either that or *he* was crazy.

No time to puzzle it out, because now they were already dragging him toward the tree. Staring up, he saw a Klansman standing beside it, his hands busily tying the final knot of a noose. Now he tossed the loose end of the heavy rope over a hanging tree limb. As his captors on either side pushed Bill forward, the man with the noose advanced, holding it out, ready to encircle his neck.

Bill twisted his head to avoid the descending loop, then lifted his right foot. Lunging sideways, he kicked out at the leg of the man at his right.

With a gasp of pain the hooded Klansman staggered off balance, stumbling against the blazing cross. His gasp turned into a scream as his robe caught fire.

Howling, he hurled himself to the ground, writhing and rolling in a frantic effort to extinguish the flame. Shouts of dismay sounded as his

companions rushed forward to aid their comrade. Freed from the grip of his captors, Bill turned and plunged out of the firelit circle and into the dark woods beyond.

Hands still tied behind his back, he stumbled forward, darting between the trees at a dead run.

Amidst the outcry and confusion in the clearing behind, a shout arose to speed him on his course. "Look out! The nigger's getting away!"

Bill didn't look back. Had he done so, he might have seen one of the hooded figures hurry toward the black bulk of a pickup truck that stood parked at the far side of the clearing and hastily open its rear doors to release what waited within.

Now there was no need to look back. A sudden baying arose, telling all he needed to know.

Dogs.

They were coming after him with bloodhounds!

Bill ran faster. He weaved his way through the darkness, blundering into tree trunks. Low-hanging branches whipped his face, tangles of roots and vegetation impeded his staggering flight. Wheezing, he flung himself forward. Desperation drove him onward in response to the sound of curses and cries, the crashing of running feet, the howling of the hounds bounding behind.

Suddenly he emerged from the woods to find himself standing before the weedy edge of a riverbank. For a moment he halted there, staring down into the turbulent current glittering in the moonlight. Croaking in alarm, frightened frogs splashed into the rushing water. Bill didn't hear them; he was conscious only of the howling dogs, the whoops and shouts of the pursuing men. Someone's voice rose in a rebel yell: it seemed to come from only a few yards away.

As its echo sounded in his ear, Bill started forward. Taking a deep breath, he dived headlong into the water.

Feet thrashing, he surfaced, twisting and tugging in panic at the cord binding his wrists behind him. To his relief he felt it loosen and give way, freeing his hands. Then he began to swim downstream, moving toward the center of the rushing torrent.

Now, on the bank behind him, the dogs appeared, their howls mingling with the roar of the rushing water. A moment later they were joined by their hooded masters, armed with rifles and shotguns.

One of them called out angrily; "You won't get far, boy!"

Beside him, another hooded man cupped his hand, shouting. "You're one dead nigger! You hear me?"

A third Klansman brandished his torch, then pointed with his free hand. "There he is! I see the bastard!"

Shotguns and rifles rose, following in the direction of his outflung arm.

Bill swam forward frantically, flinching at the sound of shots whistling overhead. Filling his lungs with air, he ducked his head beneath the surface of the water. Captured by an undercurrent, his body swirled helplessly in the dark depth. Eyes bulging, lungs bursting for want of air, he bobbed to the surface again, gasping for breath.

He inhaled quickly then, tense with anticipation of the sound of gunfire. But no sound came.

No shots. No shouting. No sound of rushing water.

The river was calm.

There wasn't the slightest ripple of movement across its expanse and its surface no longer seemed clear. Instead, he found himself surrounded by floating clumps of rotting vegetation from which a brackish stench arose, steaming into the tropical night.

Tropical.

Bill glanced toward the treetops lining the shore. Their appearance was strangely altered, or changed completely. These trees seemed shorter and more compactly clustered. Ferns rose to rim the base of their gnarled trunks; tall reeds towered against the shoreline.

Dazed and bewildered, Bill swam slowly toward the riverbank at his right. Within moments his feet were touching bottom, kicking up a mixture of mud and weeds to cloud the surface of the water around him. He stood up, feeling his feet sinking into the ooze, sensing the slow swirl of the warm air against his wet skin.

And even *that* was wrong. The air was *too* warm now. Bill glanced back toward the river with a rush of recognition. It wasn't really a river at all—the look and the smell of it was more like a swamp; a tropical swamp, steaming in the humid heat of the jungle night.

But how the hell did he get here?

Bill shook his head, then froze abruptly at the sound of soft voices murmuring from the darkness of the trees lining the bank. He crouched down quickly, shielding his body behind the reed-cluster near the shore. Peering between its upthrust stalks, he watched, silent and motionless, as four uniformed men moved forth from the trees in single file. They were short and squat, with dark hair close-cropped beneath the bill-caps pushed back over perspiring foreheads. Their skin was dark and their eyes and cheekbones identified them as Orientals. All wore identical uniforms, splotched with stains of mingled mud and perspiration. In sharp contrast, the rifles they carried were spotless, the steel barrels gleaming in the moonlight.

Abruptly, Bill's memory bridged a gap of twenty years. He was just a kid then, just a young punk, drafted right out of school and into the war to kill the gooks.

Gooks!

Now he knew where he was. This was Nam, and these were Charlies—Viet Cong!

They advanced toward the riverbank still muttering softly, and for one hideous moment Bill thought they'd wade right into the water and through the weeds where he was hiding.

Then they swerved, moving left along the river's edge, following its course until they disappeared into the darkness beyond.

Bill slumped back into the water, exhausted by

his fright, his tension, his inability to comprehend what had happened.

Something stirred, rippling the surfaces surrounding him. He turned quickly, staring down in sudden terror at the sight of the green shape wriggling toward his waist. It was a watersnake and a big one.

Now, as its body twisted forward, the reptile's head drew back abruptly, jaws agape and ready to strike.

Bill hurled himself to one side and rose, stumbling and splashing through the reeds along the bank.

Then he halted as voices sounded faintly from the shore beyond. Quickly he lowered himself once again into concealment beneath the topmost level of the reeds. Even though he was soaking wet, Bill could feel the fresh perspiration trickling across his furrowed forehead.

The gooks were coming back. But now, as he hunkered down, the voices rose loud and clear. They were speaking English!

"Charlie's out there—I can hear 'em."

A deeper voice rumbled in reply. "Cool it, man! I don't hear nothing!"

A third voice sounded. "He's right—there's something moving."

Bill rose to his feet, waving his arm toward the darkened trees bordering the riverbank.

"Don't shoot!" he cried. "I'm an American! Help me—I'm hurt! Over here—"

His eyes searched the shoreline eagerly, waiting

for his rescuers to emerge from concealment behind the trees.

Nothing stirred. And now, after a moment that seemed to elongate into an eternity, he heard the voices once more. This time they dropped to a series of harsh whispers.

"What'd I tell you? They're out there all right."

"Where?"

"Too damn close for me, man."

Bill started to wade through the reeds, moving toward the shore. "Listen to me," he shouted. "I'm an American! You've got to help me—please—"

From the bank above came an excited murmur. "Look! There's one now!"

"You're right, I see him! The gook mother—"

The rest of his words were lost in the sudden burst of sound—the insane chatter of machine-gun fire.

Bill flung himself back down into the muddy waters, screaming.

"No! Don't shoot— No!"

Bullets spurted, splashing into the water around him.

Bill ducked under, holding his breath as he swam out through the shallows.

It was only when lack of air forced him to the surface that he ventured to raise his head again, gasping hoarsely as his eyes sought the shoreline.

All was silent; the firing had ceased. Once more his ears strained for sounds to break the stillness.

Frogs croaked querulously from their conceal-ment along the marshy weed-clumps bordering the riverbank. Somewhere deep in the distant jungle beyond, a night bird uttered a raucous cry.

Then, from the shadows amidst the trees bordering the shore, a murmur drifted faintly across the water. Bill recognized the voices of the patrol.

"Hear anything?"

"Not me, man. We must've got him."

Bill hesitated, fighting an impulse to call out once again. No use—those trigger-happy bastards would only start shooting again. Now all he could do was keep moving, try to get across the river. Maybe it would be safer on the other side.

He began to swim again; moving slowly, with cautious strokes in an effort to avoid disturbing the water in his progress. *Don't make waves.*

A sudden sound emerged from somewhere along the bank behind him. He halted his effort, floating on the surface as he turned his head toward shore.

The deeper voice murmured again. "What the hell's wrong with your ears? He's still swimming around out there—I heard him!"

"Nothin's wrong with my ears, man. Only thing I hear out there is frogs."

A third voice rose excitedly. "Hey, look! There's his head sticking out of the water! Bastard's trying to make it to the other side!"

Bill ducked under quickly, his arms flailing. No use worrying about the noise now. They'd spotted him, and all he could do was pray that he could stay beneath the surface long enough to reach the safety of the opposite shore. Another burst of machine-gun fire shattered the surface above his submerged head; the sound sped him on his way.

He swam on, swam until his eyes blurred, his arms ached, his lungs burned. Then, just as he reached the point of no return, his thrashing feet touched bottom.

Unable to endure another airless moment, Bill sought the surface, his head rising just far enough to clear the water. Inhaling deeply, he stared at the sheltering shore directly before him.

He'd made it!

And the gunfire from the other side of the river had ceased; now the only sounds he heard were the gasps accompanying his own intake of breath. Relieved, he drew himself up and waded through the shallows, then started up the sloping bank to head for the trees beyond.

As he did so, a shout echoed across the waters behind him.

"There he is!"

Bill turned, crouching against the side of the bank, staring back across the river. He could see the shadows of the men moving on the other side, see them all too clearly.

For the first time he realized that the river itself was not all that wide; once they started shooting again, he was done for. He crouched lower, hands digging deep into the mud as he waited for them to fire.

But no shots came. Instead, as he glanced back across the swampy stream, he saw one of the shadows raise an arm, drawing it back like a pitcher preparing to throw a ball.

Something came hurtling down from above and

landed in the mud with a dull plop, about a dozen yards to Bill's left. He turned, staring down at the object half imbedded in the soft mud of the riverbank.

This was no baseball—the size and shape were wrong. As he blinked at the reflection of its shiny surface in the moonlight, Bill heard the hissing.

Baseball? This was a grenade—

He rose, running forward.

Behind him the grenade exploded in a blinding burst of light, its blast shattering the silence. The impact of the explosion sent Bill flying, lifting him into the air to crash headfirst against the barrier of tree trunks directly before him.

He must have blacked out then; maybe for a minute, perhaps for hours. There was no way of knowing, but slowly consciousness returned.

Bill realized that he was still alive, alive and aware, lying on his back against warm grass, arms and legs outstretched. Cautiously he moved his fingers, wriggled his toes. Dull pain shot through his limbs and he felt a throbbing ache in his shoulders, but the muscles responded. He hadn't been hit after all.

Opening his eyes, he stared up past the encircling treetops toward the night sky overhead. The air above him was moist and heavy with heat. The clothing that clung to him was wet and sticky.

Nothing had changed. He was still in the jungle, still here—wherever *here* was.

Cautiously he raised himself on his right elbow and glanced back over the riverbank and the deep crater fashioned by the force of the explosion. He peered across the water. No shadow moved along the opposite shore and the only sound rising from it was the chanted litany of the frogs.

Slowly Bill rose, his eyes probing the jungle growth before him. Somewhere within its depths he could detect the drone and buzz of insects on their nocturnal rounds. There was no other sign of life.

Life?

Bill shook his head. How could he be sure that anything was alive? First those Nazis, next the Klansmen, then the gooks and the G.I.s. All of them were gone now, but had they even been real in the first place?

Maybe he was dreaming; maybe he was dying, delirious with fever. Maybe he was already dead.

But the aching in his arms and legs as he moved forward reassured him. Dead men feel no pain. Whatever had happened, wherever he was, he was still alive.

His problem now was to make sure he stayed that way.

Cautiously, eyes and ears alert for any hint of shape or sound, Bill started forward through the trees ahead. He had no hint what lay beyond the jungle; all he wanted to do was get away—away from the river, away from the shapes that prowled his nightmare.

Nightmare—that's what it was—that's what it had to be!

Nothing else made any sense to him. But if it was a nightmare, then why didn't he wake up?

And when had he fallen asleep?

He remembered being with Ray and Larry. That part was real, and he knew he wasn't asleep in the bar. But how long had it been since then?

Was it hours, days, months?

Somehow it seemed like years; yes, it had to be years, because of the Nazis. And when had the Ku Klux Klan stopped lynching niggers? That was years ago, too, and so was the war in Nam.

Bill shook his head. How could it be years ago? It was still going on, and he was in Nam now. Here, in the middle of the night, lost in the jungle.

This was no dream; he could smell the rot, feel sweat break out over his body in the humid heat of the tropical night, feel the stinging of the mosquito swarms surrounding him, hear their angry buzzing as he advanced.

Advanced?

Bill halted, glancing around him at the trees, which loomed in silent circles.

Which way was he going? How could he be sure he was moving in the right direction? There was no trail to follow, nothing to see but the trees stretching endlessly on all sides.

He was lost, lost in the jungle. His lips moved in a silent prayer; *Please, God, help me. Get me out of here!*

There was no answer, no sign; only the insect-humming rising from the tangle of vines and creepers looping snakelike between the tree trunks.

For a moment longer, Bill stood indecisively, then turned abruptly to his right and began to move forward again. Keep moving, that was the answer. *God helps those who help themselves.*

His entire body was aching now; he felt like he'd been beaten with a sledgehammer, but he kept going, had to keep going, because there was no other choice. Sooner or later he'd get to the end of this jungle and come out on the other side. No way of knowing what he'd find there, but anything was better than this maze of darkness in which he floundered.

Tripping over vines, blundering into overhanging branches, slapping at the insects that assailed him, Bill panted forward.

Then, suddenly, the way ahead was clear.

Halting at the edge of the clearing, he glanced down at the river below. Bill shook his head, his jaw muscles tightening.

Oh no—don't tell me I doubled back!

Another glance reassured him, however, that the stream was broader and wider than the one he had crossed. And rising behind the bank on the opposite side was a towering cliff. At its base was a cluster of thatch-roofed structures, perhaps a dozen or so. Light bulbs loosely strung on wires hung between the huts, and in their glare he could see a black cluster of insects encircling each bulb with a dark and humming halo. The light was reflected on the surface of the water below, flecking its murkiness with glints of gold.

Bill stood silent, focusing eyes and ears intently. But nothing moved beneath the light on the other side and no sound broke the stillness. Even the frogs were silent here.

Slowly, he started down the sloping bank to the

water's edge, glancing left and right as he did so. In the jungle growth behind him the mosquitoes' hum was faintly audible. That was all he heard. Before him the river stretched soundless, its surface serene.

Bill made his way to the water's edge, staring into the lighted semicircle of huts once again.

Again his eyes searched for a hint of movement, and again he hesitated.

Had the villagers seen him? Were they hiding from him in fear or had they retreated into the huts to surprise him with an ambush?

There was no way of telling, no way of knowing if he faced friend or foe. Only the lights held promise, beckoning him forward, out of the darkness. No matter what might be lurking across the river, it was better than what lay behind him.

Bill waded into the water and when it rose to waist-level he started to swim, ignoring his body's aching protest. No matter how tired he was, he had to keep going.

To his surprise, as he swam he felt the tension in his muscles ebbing, but the realization was purely physical; his mind was not affected.

Or was it? Once again the events of the past few hours flashed before him and again the question came: Had it only been hours? Suddenly it seemed to him that he'd been on the run forever—running from the Nazis, the Klansmen, then those G.I.s in the jungle. Had it really happened or was he going crazy?

The full ache in his limbs returned and now he

greeted it gratefully; at least this gave him part of the answer. There was no way he could be so beat unless what had happened was real.

It wasn't his imagination and he wasn't crazy. It was the others who'd freaked out; the Nazis who mistook him for a Jew, the Klansmen who thought he had nigger blood, the G.I.s who figured him for a gook.

What was the matter with them, didn't they have eyes? Couldn't they see that he was an American all along? If they'd only looked, only listened, they should have known.

Crazy, that's what they were. But it didn't matter now; the important thing was that he'd escaped and if he could find someone here in the village across the river, if they were friendly, then maybe they'd help him to get away. Away from the jungle and the crazies, help him to get back home again.

Reaching the shallows, Bill rose to his feet and made his way to shore. Ahead of him the hanging lights still burned, but nothing stirred in the shadows beyond.

Again the thought came and with it rose the fear: Was it an ambush?

There was only one way to find out, and now that he was here he had to take the chance. Slowly he forced himself forward up the bank and stepped into the semicircular clearing before the thatched huts arranged by the cliffside. Above him he could hear the buzz and drone of the insects fluttering around the burning bulbs. There was no other sound except his own harsh breathing and the muffled thudding of his heartbeat.

Outlined against the light, Bill glanced across the compound. What were they waiting for? If they had weapons, now was the time to use them; standing here he made a perfect target. And if they didn't shoot, if they were friendly, then why were they afraid to show themselves?

Bill swallowed quickly, then took a deep breath. "Anybody here?" he shouted.

The only answer was the echo of his own voice.

Bill frowned. Maybe they couldn't understand what he was saying, but at least they had heard him call out and they could see he was unarmed. Why didn't they show themselves?

Still no sound, still no movement, except for that of insects buzzing and fluttering around the bare bulbs overhead.

Bill turned and crossed to the hut on the far end at his left. He moved along the side to the open doorway, halting there. Again he called. "Anybody here? Come on out— It's all right, I won't hurt you."

There was no answer to his invitation. Beyond the darkened doorway, all was still.

Bill took a step forward, then peered into the hut. Dimly he discerned the cast-iron cookstove in one corner, the sleeping-mats littering the bare earth on either side. Other than that, the hut was empty.

Frowning, he started around the semicircle, pausing to peer through each doorway in turn, finding nothing but a duplication of the first hut's contents. Stove and sleeping-mats . . . and in a few cases, bowls and cooking utensils, plus a few blankets and bundles of clothing. Behind him the lights still blazed and in several of the huts he noted the presence of cooking pots atop the stoves.

He stepped inside to examine one of them, starring down at the bubbling broth and sniffing its aroma.

There must have been someone here quite recently, that much was certain. And it looked as though they'd left in a hurry; that much was obvious, too, but where had they gone? And why had they left in such a hurry?

Bill stumbled out of the hut, staring around the deserted village and shaking his head. No sense trying to figure out what had happened here; all he knew was that he was still alone, alone and tired. Tired of thinking, tired of running. All he wanted now was sleep; yet deep within him, a warning sounded. He couldn't afford to fall asleep, not here, not now. But he had to get some rest.

Moving around to the side of the hut, Bill lowered himself to the ground and leaned back against the outer wall, surrendering to the wave of weariness that rose within him. Involuntarily his eyes closed. Now the wave crested, drowning him in darkness.

Drowning, that's what he was doing now.

He had to be drowning, going down for the third time because his whole life passed in review. The inner visions flashed before him: Ray and Larry needling him in the bar—the Nazi officers shooting as he raced across the rooftops—his fall to the pavement below. Now the Klansmen were dangling the noose before his neck—again he forced one of his hooded captors against the fiery cross, hearing him scream in agony. Suddenly the scream was transformed into the baying of the bloodhounds pursuing him through the night—then their howling was lost in the stutter of the machine gun and the rumbling roar of the exploding grenade. Once more he blundered blindly through the jungle, swam the river, searched the silent huts—

Bill's eyes blinked open.

For a moment he didn't know where he was, but as his vision cleared, he stared up at the dangling lights and into the darkness beyond.

He realized that he must have fallen asleep in spite of himself; he'd been dreaming, but now he was fully awake, fully aware.

Bill turned, glancing toward the river. The black bulk of a catamaran loomed from the center of the stream, its unfurled sails offering ample explanation of how it achieved its silent approach.

In the dimness Bill could discern the movement of shadowy shapes at the stern of the craft.

Bill rose, racing toward the shelter of the undergrowth beyond the far end of the compound.

Up ahead, just past the end of the hut farthest to his right, he caught a glimpse of a narrow path half-hidden by overhanging shrubbery. He ran for it quickly, disappearing beneath the shelter of its branches. Panting, he paused, staring back toward the river.

Now the catamaran was dark no longer; sweeping forward from its back, the beam of a powerful spotlight fanned across the huddle of huts in search of the fugitive.

He started up along the narrow pathway that snaked through the underbrush covering the steeply slanted cliffside.

Panting, Bill clambered forward. The path was steep; he toiled upward, puffing and sweating with the intensity of his efforts.

Now a shell whistled behind him and burst against the side of the path below.

Turning, Bill glanced down past the conflagration of the compound. The river was red in the reflection of the flames and on its crimson surface a small boat bobbed, pulling away from the catamaran and moving toward the shore. Bill scowled, watching it approach the beach below.

They were sending a landing party!

Frantically, he labored up the path to the shelter of the trees surmounting the cliff top.

Now, from far below, Bill heard shouts rising over the roar of the flames.

He started forward again, eyes alert, seeking an opening through the trees ahead.

Then he saw it—the small wooden shed standing unobtrusively in the deeper shadows at his left.

He ran toward the entrance, his hand moving quickly toward the door.

To his relief it swung inward. He stumbled across the threshold. Then he halted, staring through the shadows of the shed's interior. Piles of kindling surrounded him on three sides, leaving only a narrow space between as he closed the door. In the darkness he groped forward, reaching out to dislodge a length of cordwood at the right. Blindly he began to pile logs against the door, working feverishly to raise an improvised barrier.

Then, he huddled down in the darkness. There was nothing else he could do now except pray that somehow his hiding place would pass unnoticed once the landing party reached the top of the cliff.

For a long moment Bill crouched there, listening intently for a sound from beyond the barricaded door. The shelling had ceased and the distant crackle of flames diminished. Bill waited now for the sound of voices and footsteps to signal the landing party's approach.

Nothing stirred in the silence of the night beyond.

Bill felt a sudden surge of relief. Perhaps his escape route hadn't been discovered. Once the landing party searched the burning village and found nothing, it would return to the boat, leaving him here in safety.

Dear God, Bill prayed silently. Let them go—go away and leave me in peace—

But now, suddenly, he heard the howling.

Rising through the night came the baying of hounds, and over it the shouts sounding directly before the door.

To his horror, he recognized familiar voices, whooping in triumph.

"We got us a nigger in the woodpile!"

"Yippee! Let's burn him out!"

"No way—I want him alive. Hang on to them dogs until we get that door down!"

The Ku Klux Klan again!

But how could they be here?

Numb with bewilderment, frozen with fear, Bill listened as the door of the shed began to splinter beneath the blows of an axe blade.

He rose, reaching for a piece of cordwood from the pile at his right. But before his hand closed around it, the door crashed inward.

The Nazi soldiers grabbed Bill by the shoulder, knocking the wood from his hand, and pulled him out of the shed.

Nazis? How did they get here?

And where was he?

The cliff top and the burning village below had vanished. He was standing on cobblestones again, standing on the rain-swept platform of a railroad depot, in broad daylight, surrounded by uniformed men, his arms pinned behind his back. There were no hounds, no hooded figures. Struggling, he turned his head to catch a glimpse of the shed behind him. It too had changed; instead of huddling alone beneath the trees, it appeared to be attached to the side of the depot.

Now the soldier dragged him forward to confront the Nazi officer standing motionless on the platform in the driving rain.

Bill shouted at him. "Let me go!"

The officer's voice rose in harsh command. Bill's captors shoved him toward the depot wall.

Desperately, Bill jerked his head around, glancing back at the cordon of soldiers standing behind their leader. "What's happening to me?" he panted.

The soldiers stood stiffly at attention, unmindful of the man, unmindful of his voice.

Bill closed his eyes. Maybe he was seeing things, hallucinating again. Yes, that had to be the answer; all this was imagination, and if he'd just get a grip on himself, it would go away. *Easy does it now. Count to ten, take a deep breath, and when you open your eyes, you'll be back in the shed again—*

He started to inhale, but the breath burst from his body as he was slammed against the bricks of the depot wall.

Depot?

Bill's eyes blinked open and the despairing realization came that nothing had changed; he was still here, his outstretched arms gripped by the soldiers. And now, advancing toward him through the rain, the Nazi officer reached into his jacket and dangled an object before him.

Bill stared at the piece of yellow cloth cut in the shape of a star—the Star of David.

Reaching out, the officer pinned the emblem on Bill's chest. Turning, he nodded toward the squad of men standing at attention, rifle barrels gleaming in the rain. *"Hier ist nur ein auderen."* He gestured toward Bill. *"Stell ihn mit den anderen."*

As the squad started toward him, Bill lunged forward, breaking free from the grip of his captors on either side. "I'm an American citizen," he panted. "Don't you understand?"

One of the soldiers detached himself from the squad; without breaking his stride, he raised his rifle and clubbed Bill across the side of the head.

Dazed, Bill fell face forward on the wet cobblestones. Pain surged through him, but somehow he managed to find his voice again. "I won't let you do this to me," he murmured.

Clutching hands pulled him upright, dragged him across the depot platform. Opening his eyes, Bill stared at the long line of freight cars standing on the tracks. All of them were sealed shut except for the one directly before him. Guards stood beside it with rifles raised, their bayonets jabbing at the shadowy figures filling the doorway above.

Bill turned to the soldier on his left, eyes pleading. "No—please—You're making a mistake—"

Suddenly he felt himself being lifted from behind. Thrust forward through the opened doorway, he landed heavily, lurching against the packed bodies of the other occupants. Someone grabbed his arm, helping him to regain his balance. Glancing around, he scanned the faces of his fellow prisoners. Some were young, some were old, but all bore identical looks of resignation and despair; and like himself, all wore the yellow star.

With a rumble, the sliding door of the freight car clanged shut. Cries of fear rose in response behind him.

As the train clanked forward, Bill collapsed against the side of the car, listening to the screams and wails of the helpless horde surrounding him, and the relentless clatter of the wheels against the tracks.

Bill knew where he was going now, knew what would happen when he got there, and yet somehow it didn't matter. What happened to him wasn't important.

He would die, the others would die, and in time the Nazis would die. It was all the same, both for victims and for victors. And it would always be the same until the day when hatred would die too. *Bill's lips moved in a silent prayer as the train rumbled through the twilight.*

2

VALENTINE

The plane plunged into the twilight.

From his window-seat just forward of the right wing, Mr. Valentine blinked out at the darkening sky. Then, frowning, he consulted his wristwatch.

Three o'clock. Too early, much too early for twilight. And yet, the clouds encircling the aircraft were violet, almost purple. Peering ahead, Valentine noted a deepening darkness beyond. His frown deepened in response.

Thunderclouds?

Oh no, not that. It couldn't be. Not after the way he'd checked the weather reports in the morning paper. Clear skies all the way—that's what the map showed and only fifteen minutes ago the captain's voice had crackled a cheery greeting over the intercom, announcing the promise of a smooth on-course flight at an altitude of thirty-five thousand feet.

Sorry, Captain. I don't like your altitude. And your prediction is for the birds.

Or would be, if there were any birds. But birds were too smart to venture up to that height. Only a fool would take such a risk, and only a damned fool would put his faith in the smarmy reassurance of a pilot who was paid to offer it to a captive audience of passengers.

Surely the captain must have seen the cloud banks ahead. Unless, of course, he was blind. In which case he shouldn't be flying.

And neither should I, Valentine told himself.

But there was no help for it. The conference opened tomorrow morning and neither automobile nor Amtrak could cross the continent in eighteen hours. He'd asked for a week off in advance with the thought in mind—either driving or taking the train—but his production supervisor had vetoed that idea in a hurry.

"Sorry, no way. We're working shorthanded as it is, and you've got that Carver job to finish up before you go. Why waste all that time when you can hop on a plane Thursday afternoon and still get a good night's rest before Friday's program starts? I mean, what's your problem?"

I'm scared spitless, that's the problem. Only Valentine couldn't tell him that. *My God, it's been eighty years since the Wright Brothers took off at Kitty Hawk, and nobody's afraid of flying anymore.*

A glance around the cabin confirmed Valentine's thought. There were two stewardesses up front near the galley—one quite young and the other in her thirties—chatting calmly together, smiling as if they didn't have a care in the world. But of course they'd be calm. Even if they weren't, they'd *look* calm; that was part of their job.

The passengers seemed to be calm, too. As a matter of fact, most of them had turned off their reading lamps and were dozing. In one of the seats ahead, an enormous man had assumed the fetal position; a fat baby, with his head resting against the window. Nearby, a young couple reclined in entwined embrace. An elderly couple across the aisle from them slept without touching one another, their indifference born of long association. In the seat directly before him, a mother sat beside a little girl, her impassivity a sharp contrast to her daughter's wriggling. No one seemed troubled by the slight rocking motion of the plane or by the presence of the purple clouds gathering beyond the window.

So why was he upset? Valentine frowned. Obviously there was no sense trying to rest—the way he felt, sleep was out of the question. But perhaps work might spell salvation. He reached up and turned on the reading lamp, pulled out his tray table. Groping into his opened briefcase on the empty seat beside him, Valentine produced the tools of his trade—a note pad, a pocket calculator, and a textbook. He opened the volume to a page indicated by a bookmark and concentrated on the array of equations thus revealed. Taking a ball-point pen from his breast pocket, he unscrewed the cap and held the point over the blank note pad. For a moment he stared at the letters and numerals on the page of the textbook, only to find his eyes blurring.

Valentine blinked, but his vision did not clear. Neither did his thoughts. How could a man put his mind to math, concentrate on abstract theory, in the midst of menacing reality? And the reality was all around him; the reality of shuddering motion, the reality of swollen storm clouds just beyond the windowpane.

Valentine put down his pen and shut the book, but he couldn't shut out his thoughts. Perhaps it was time to face the truth. Just what was there about flying that troubled him so greatly? Where did his exaggerated dislike of air travel come from?

Could it be the commercials? Even when sitting in the security of his own home, with no seat belts trapping him into his easy chair, he had always been conscious of a vague irritation when confronted by the paeans of praise for flight, which emanated from his television screen. All those images of scenic grandeur and jumbo jets sailing serenely through the blue and cloudless skies over shining seas—all those unseen heavenly choirs chanting about the high adventure and low fares to be found in the skies—what nonsense! Most of the flights he had taken offered nothing of visual grandeur; what he usually saw from his window were clouds and smog, or a combination of both. And the fare-structure had always been a source of irritation to him. It seemed to turn out that so-called bargain rates were offered only to family groups traveling at some ungodly hour of the night to one of a very few major cities. The moment you embarked on a journey at a sensible hour, traveling alone, the rates escalated to astronomical proportions. Why did it cost $99 to fly three thousand miles across the country as opposed to $400 or $500 for a journey one-third that distance? No matter how loudly the choir sang or how often the offscreen announcer boasted of bargains—fair or unfair—Valentine always seemed to end up trapped in a situation like this.

Trapped.

That was the operative word. The whole trip was a trap. That's how you started—trapped in a tangle of traffic as you approached the airport. Trapped in a maze of jammed parking lots. Trapped in a staggering, stumbling dash from lot to terminal, hefting the bulky burden of your luggage. Trapped in the line waiting at the passenger counter. Trapped in the anxiety of anticipation once you reached it: Were your tickets in order? Was your flight departing on time? Could you be certain, once you checked in, that your luggage would be put through to its proper destination?

Then, of course, there was the business of passing through the security check. The X-ray eye scrutinizing the contents of your hand-luggage was bad enough, but the cold, fishy stare of the security people was even worse. Foolish, of course, but Valentine always went through the procedure with the feelings of a felon; the whole thing reminded him all too vividly of police procedure. He half expected one of the uniformed guards to grab him by the collar with a curt command: *"Up against the wall, clasp both hands behind your head. It is my duty to warn you that you have the right to remain silent; anything you say may be used in evidence."*

Then there was a long walk to the terminal gate, the endless plodding through the white-walled corridor under the harsh glare of fluorescent illumination. *The last mile.*

Only worse. At least the prisoner condemned to execution could expect to reach his destination and pass through the little green door without interruption. But air terminal procedure was different. Once at the gate, you stood in line again, waiting for the door to open. From overhead came the canned cacophony of tape recordings, punctuated abruptly by an announcer squawking static-riddled gibberish, which involuntarily evoked one's nerve-racked attention. Would your name be called to report to the nearest telephone? Was your flight going to be delayed for an extra hour? Standing before the departure gate was always an ordeal, and even if you could disregard what issued overhead, there was no way to ignore the presence of your fellow prisoners. Correction—fellow passengers. But as far as Valentine was concerned, he heartily wished that those passengers had been in prison. Perhaps he was squeamish; he preferred to think of himself merely as a private person who lacked the normal quotient of gregariousness. Whatever it was, he disliked the close proximity of young mothers with squalling infants in their arms or the overweight oldsters who seemed to think it necessary to embark on a flight to Philadelphia wearing cowboy hats with brims pulled down to shadow their fat, bespectacled faces. Again, at least the condemned man is granted the privilege of taking his seat in the electric chair alone; he doesn't have to put up with the indignity of a crying baby seated beside him, or the presence of one of those pseudo-cowboys who will talk him to death during the journey into oblivion. Better to suffer the brief pain of electrocution than the endless agony of elocution.

Valentine sighed softly. This was nit-picking, he knew, over-dramatization. All he was doing was trying to forestall the ultimate reality—the fear that possessed him after the waiting interval at the terminal—the terminal illness, ending when he finally boarded his flight.

Again, the situation contrasted unfavorably with that of a condemned prisoner. When they put you in the electric chair, you at least have the comfort of knowing that you don't have to lay out an exorbitant sum—to say nothing of an exorbitant tax—to pay for your seat; and no one sentenced to death is expected to strap himself into the hot seat. He doesn't have to sit there in endless anticipation of what is to come; he doesn't have to listen to the sound of the engines revving up and wonder whether or not they seem to be in proper working order. He doesn't have to endure the long, slow, bumpy shudder of movement as the plane heads into position for its takeoff at a distant runway. He doesn't face the repetition of the engines' roaring, followed by the thrust of acceleration as the plane suddenly swoops forward with a surge of shrieking sound as it seeks to rise.

And when it does finally rise, when one is conscious of being airborne at last, there is always the clamor of one's inner voice: Will it clear those damned power lines just beyond the airport boundaries? Will it manage to soar above the high-rises of the city streets or the mountains ringing the desert location—or the roaring waters of an ocean takeoff? And what about that dangerously steep slanting of wings when the aircraft swerves, as it inevitably seems to do, before heading into the flight-path?

Naturally, these questions are never voiced, let alone answered, in the little recitation that a bored stewardess hastily delivers prior to takeoff. *Fasten your seat belts . . . place your seat in the upright position . . . extinguish all smoking materials . . . blah, blah, blah, oxygen mask overhead, blah, blah, blah, emergency exits . . .* Valentine could almost recite the standard reassurances from memory, but there was no point to it, because they were meaningless.

How many times had that same speech been made just before a takeoff where the plane did *not* clear the wires, or the buildings, or the mountaintop, or the surface of the sea? How many times had the mechanical reassurance been given before an aircraft started to bank, only to spin into the spiral of a fatal crash? Once you hit the power line or the jutting obstacle ahead, it didn't much matter whether or not the oxygen mask descended on schedule; and the emergency exits offered no escape from the fiery explosion.

Valentine shifted in his seat. Why was he wasting his time with such morbidities? He'd already gone the route; run the gauntlet of traffic and terminal, endured the anticipatory dread of waiting and survived the perils, real and imaginary, of the takeoff. So why was he still uptight now?

Then realization came. It wasn't fear of danger that produced his palpitations of mind and body. The real terror came from the realization of his helplessness.

Here he was, sailing along serenely at an elevation of thirty-five thousand feet. The FASTEN YOUR SEAT BELTS sign had blinked off, and nicotine-addicts were free to risk lung cancer again. The stewardesses would go into the galley soon to load the refreshment cart, and up front, behind the closed door sealing off the nose of the plane, the pilot and his crew were huddled over their instrument panels.

Or were they? For all he knew, they might be discussing this afternoon's football games, or last night's adventures on the town. Somewhere Valentine had read that employees of flight crews were instructed not to indulge in alcohol or any form of dissipation for twenty-four hours prior to a scheduled assignment. But how could you be certain they'd followed those instructions? There were also those reassuring public-relations statements about mandatory regular physical checkups for all flight personnel, but again, there was always the random factor of unpredictability. Suddenly he remembered an episode in his own family history—how Uncle Joe had gone in for his usual annual physical checkup and emerged from the doctor's office with a clean bill of health, only to drop dead of cardiac arrest in the elevator that was taking him down to the street. Good old Uncle Joe—only forty-eight years old, pink of condition, best damned tennis player in the annual competition at the country club. No smoking, no drinking, no doping, no womanizing—but suddenly, without warning, no heartbeat. If it could happen to his Uncle Joe going down in an elevator, it sure as hell could happen to somebody else's uncle going up in an aircraft. The difference being that when Uncle Joe's heart gave out, the elevator didn't crash.

For God's sake, Valentine told himself, *stop acting like a baby! Try to think of something else.*

And so he did. He thought about air pockets—unexpected wind currents that could envelop the plane suddenly, without warning, and hurl it to destruction below. He thought about wind-shears that crumpled wings and turned jumbo jets into helpless insects unable to withstand the buffeting of a storm.

Valentine blinked and jerked erect at the sudden glimpse of green slashing through the sky beyond the window.

Lightning.

He'd been right about the presence of the storm ahead. Only it wasn't ahead anymore; they were actually into it now. The skies beyond the windows were almost black and raindrops spattered against the glass.

The plane bounced into a sickening lurch and so did Valentine's stomach.

Glancing down, he noted that his hands were gripping the edges of his armrest.

White knuckles. How he hated that casually used slang phrase! But his knuckles *were* white and he was pretty damned sure that his face was turning green.

Better find out about that. As plane and stomach wrenched again, Valentine released his grip on the armrest and scooped up the objects on his tray table, depositing them in the briefcase. Pushing the table up and securing it in position against the back of the seat directly ahead of him, he rose and made his way down the aisle in the direction of the lavatory. Two stewardesses were in the galley now and neither of them—a rather attractive young girl and her somewhat older companion—noticed him as he moved past and entered the lavatory on his left.

The cubicle was small and dark, like an upright coffin, but when the door closed behind him, the fluorescence flickered on. Valentine found himself facing the washstand mirror and there his worst fears were confirmed. His face *did* have a greenish cast. He stared at his reflection, noting the telltale terror in his eyes. Confronting his countenance, he found the final fear. Helplessness was not the ultimate horror, nor was the fear of flying. The thing that really got to him was the fear of *falling*.

God knows where it started, or when: probably in infancy. As far back as he could remember he was aware of that particular phobia, both in waking life and in his all-too-vivid dreams. It was in those dreams, dreams that survived into adulthood, that he would suddenly find himself dropping down into darkness—deep, deep darkness, like that of the storm clouds outside the plane. There were no windows in the lavatory and he couldn't see the sky here, but he could feel the force of the storm that surged around the aircraft. The wrenches came faster now, quickening in a regular rhythm. A tiny light flickered on behind the lettered inscription: PLEASE RETURN TO YOUR SEAT.

Valentine ignored it. But he couldn't ignore the mounting panic.

Once again he faced himself in the mirror, trying to ignore the too-bright terror in his eyes. *Take a good look at yourself. You're a grown man; a computer analyst and a damned good one. You of all people should be comfortable around advanced technology. Well, those people up there in the nose*

*of this plane are knowledgeable, too. They have
their own expertise. There must be hundreds of
flights that encounter storms and air turbulence
every day and pass through safely. Why should this
one be different?*

But he still was facing the question. Why was he
so afraid of falling? Was he crazy? Or was all this
the result of some trauma he'd pushed back into the
unconscious? Maybe his mother may have acciden-
tally dropped him as a baby.

If so, she must have dropped you on your head,
Valentine told himself.

The plane lurched again and Valentine felt his
gut respond in sympathy, but sympathy wouldn't
help him now; not the way he was breathing. For
the first time, he realized that the sound he had
vaguely noted over the drone of the engines was
emanating from his own mouth. He wasn't just
breathing hard, he was gasping—hyperventilating.
It wasn't a new experience and he knew what to do.
Valentine reached into the slot beneath the washbasin and pulled out a barf bag. He yanked it open,
lowered himself to the toilet seat and began to
breathe into the receptacle. Suddenly he looked up
at the sound of a *ping*. The light above the
washbasin flashed again.

PLEASE RETURN TO YOUR SEAT.

Another *ping* and then the crackle of a voice on
the intercom:

"This is Captain Deveraux. Folks, I'd like you to
buckle up snugly in your seat belt and extinguish
your smoking materials. We have a little unfriendly

weather up ahead and we just might bounce around for a bit."

Now he tells us. Valentine grimaced wryly and started to raise the paper bag to his mouth and nose again.

Another *ping* interrupted him. This time the voice of one of the stewardesses came over the intercom:

"We'll be suspending our in-flight service for a few minutes. For those of you still waiting for refreshment, we'll get back to you as soon as we're through the turbulence."

To hell with refreshments. Valentine raised the bag once more, only to halt at the sound of a knock on the lavatory door. The muffled voice of the stewardess was faintly audible: "Please get back to your seat as soon as you can."

Valentine opened his mouth to reply but nothing came out but a hoarse gasp.

The plane bucked violently. Valentine's right elbow knocked violently against the edge of the washstand. But the knock outside the door was more violent still.

Again he heard the voice of the stewardess: "Hello in there! Can you hear me? Helloooo!"

Valentine ignored her as he buried his face in the folds of the open bag, concentrating on regulating his breathing. During the moment of merciful silence from the passageway outside the door, he managed to regain control and regulate his respiration.

Then the knocking resumed, in a series of sharp

staccato raps. The voice accompanying it held a note of shrill urgency:

"Mr. Valentine? Can I help you? *Mr. Valentine!*"

This time Valentine managed a reply. "Just a minute—I'll be right out."

Rising, he stood swaying before the mirror. His color looked better now—the greenish tinge had disappeared—but he still felt faint. Turning on the tap and gripping the knob firmly to maintain the water's reluctant flow, he splashed his face with his free hand. Through the door the stewardess's voice sounded again:

"I'll help you to your seat."

"One moment," Valentine called. "Just a moment."

Moment of decision, Valentine told himself. Reluctantly he dipped his hand into his left jacket pocket and pulled out a small, plastic pillbox. Fumbling with the catch, he opened the container and dumped its contents into his palm—two blue Valiums and a Dramamine. As he stared at the pills, his resolution firmed. He knew what to expect if he swallowed all three of the capsules, but what the hell—better to be a walking zombie than the totally lifeless victim of a heart attack. Taking a deep breath, he gulped down the pills.

Pulling a paper cup from the wall-container, he filled it with water for a chaser. Swallowing, he glanced again into the mirror. The floor of the plane beneath his feet lurched sickeningly and the mirror image distorted in accompaniment to his own grimace. Groaning, he closed his eyes and turned, fumbling for the door latch.

The door opened and so did his eyes. The countenance he presented to the waiting stewardess was perfectly calm.

But from her own expression, she wasn't buying it. He recognized that I've-been-here-before look in her smile.

"I know how you feel, Mr. Valentine." Her voice sounded softly over the tortured throbbing of the plane's engines. "Lots of people are uptight about flying when the weather gets a little rough. Just try to remember that statistically it's safer up here than on the ground—safer even than your own bathroom."

Spare me the lavatory humor. Valentine forced a response to her smile. "I'm fine," he told her. "Perfectly fine."

The plane bounced again, and suddenly Valentine lost his balance, colliding against the stewardess. As he made contact with the C-cupped contour of her breasts, he froze and drew back quickly. The younger stewardess was standing behind her companion and now she made her presence known with a laugh.

"Whoops!" She approached, gripping his left arm. "Let's get you back to your seat."

The older stewardess reached out to grasp his right arm and the two women started to propel him past the galley entryway.

Valentine stifled a groan, but not the thought which prompted it. *Jesus, they're treating me like a basket case! You'd think I was ninety years old. But if those damned pills would only start working, I'll bet I wouldn't feel a day over eighty.*

Proceeding down the aisle, he noticed that his fellow passengers were no longer asleep. The buffeting of the storm had brought rude awakenings to the fat man, the old couple, and their younger counterparts. Only the woman whom he guessed to be the mother of the wriggling little girl still rested with her eyes closed.

He hoped to God that others farther back in the cabin hadn't awakened. The way these idiots here watched his progress made him doubly self-conscious; he must look like some kind of a nut lurching along in the custody of his two uniformed attendants.

He settled down into his seat, uneasily aware that the stewardesses were still hovering over him. The older of the two was eyeing his face for telltale signs of stress, but the younger one directed her attention to the empty seat beside him, where his briefcase rested. Following her glance, he discovered that it rested no longer. The jolting of the plane had toppled it over on its side and its contents were now strewn across the surface of the seat—note pad, calculator, and the textbook.

The young stewardess squinted down at the opened title page. *"Micro Chip Logic—The Liberation of the Left Brain."* She smiled at him. "You're a science fiction fan, huh?"

"It's a textbook," Valentine told her. "Computers."

The young stewardess gave him a questioning glance. "You really *read* this stuff?"

"I wrote it," Valentine murmured.

The girl checked the title page again. "My goodness, so you did." She smiled at her older companion. "How about that?"

Ignoring her, the senior stewardess addressed Valentine. "Very impressive. But why don't we put it away now and try to get some sleep?"

Valentine's inward groan echoed again. *What gives? First they act as if I were an old man, and now they're treating me like a kid.*

He left the thought unspoken, but now, as the younger stewardess reached up and turned off his reading lamp, he found his voice. "No—please don't. I'd rather have the light on."

The girl shrugged and switched the light back on, then turned and made her way along the aisle. The senior stewardess remained poised beside Valentine's seat, peering down at his face. For a moment she studied it, then came to a decision. She bent forward to speak, her low murmur scarcely audible above the whine of the engines.

"Mr. Valentine—we're not supposed to do this, but I have these sedatives—" Reaching into her jacket pocket, she brought out a small bottle, carefully concealing it in the palm of her hand as she continued. "They might help you get some rest."

Valentine shook his head quickly. "No thanks."

"They're very mild," she persisted.

Valentine forced a smile of reassurance. "I'll be fine—really I will."

He blinked, startled at the sudden flash of light from above the back of the seat directly before him.

Now a diminutive head popped up over the seat back. Valentine recognized the face of the little girl as she grinned down at him, one hand gripping the seat for support and the other brandishing a piece of exposed film. Then he realized—the kid had taken the photograph with her Polaroid.

The little girl dangled the developing snapshot before them and her grin broadened. "This will cost you four bucks," she said.

"What?" The senior stewardess offered her a perplexed frown.

"Only kidding," the girl giggled.

"Come along," said the stewardess, moving forward to take the girl's arm. "No more pictures. You're supposed to be buckled down next to your mommy."

Valentine watched as she ushered the protesting youngster back to her seat beside her dozing mother across the aisle. Reluctantly the child secured her seat belt while the stewardess waited. Then she turned back to Valentine.

"I'm Susan St. John. If you need anything, just call for me."

Valentine shook his head, forcing another fixed smile. "Thank you again. But don't worry, I'm all right now, truly I am."

The stewardess nodded and started off. Her movement left the aisle vacant and revealed the face of the little girl in the seat directly across from him. She wasn't grinning now, just staring at him—and what in the hell was this thing she was holding up for his inspection? A doll wearing a striped jacket and a straw hat—a doll with the face of W. C. Fields! Valentine blinked. No, it wasn't a doll—more like a ventriloquist's dummy.

The little girl's face remained impassive but the dummy peered at him with an ugly crooked grin of its own.

Christ! It was bad enough having all these people looking at him without putting up with a dummy too. And that goddam grin was just too much—

Valentine turned away, his breath rasping a warning. Better not get worked up or he'd start hyperventilating again. He fumbled in his right-hand pocket and pulled a cigarette loose from its pack. Placing it between his lips, he sent his hand on an errand into the pocket once more, this time to bring out a matchbook.

Striking a match on its surface, he cupped his palms and bent forward to get a light—then jerked his head up at the sound of a shrill whistle.

Turning, he stared at the little girl across the aisle. Her face was still impassive, but W. C. Fields suddenly jerked one of his arms up toward the lighted sign overhead. A squeaky mock-adult voice seemed to issue from the grin-distorted mouth.

"You heard the captain. *No* smoking!"

The little girl's expression was unchanged. For a moment Valentine found himself half believing that the dummy had actually spoken.

Again the voice sounded—this time louder, more emphatic.

"N-O! No smoking!"

Now the fat man occupying the seat in front of her turned and glared at Valentine. From the seats behind his own, occupied by the elderly couple, an old lady's voice rose shrilly:

"He ought to have more respect for his body!"

Valentine extinguished the flickering flame, then dropped the match into his ashtray, followed by his cigarette.

Across the aisle, the little girl closed her eyes with a smile of satisfaction. Clasping the dummy in her arm, she lay back, prepared to sleep. The fat man turned his glance away and from behind Valentine's seat there was only silence.

Valentine's breathing slowed. Thank God that was over with! Now all was still except for the persistent roar of the engines. Perhaps if they'd only leave him alone, he might actually be able to get some sleep, too. Those pills should be working by now. He sank back, closing his eyes.

The drone of the engines deepened and so did the darkness behind his lowered lids. But the darkness wasn't empty. Far in the distance a faint speck of light glimmered. He found himself following its movements as it fluttered erratically with the fitfulness of a firefly. And like a firefly, its glow grew stronger as it approached.

Only then did Valentine realize that what now loomed luminescently before him was neither light nor insect—it was the face of the dummy.

The open mouth moved, articulating a hoarse command:

"Please return to your grave! Extinguish all life! This is your captain shrieking—"

Now it was Valentine's turn to open his mouth, but no shriek sounded in response. All he heard was a faint dry rasping deep in his own throat—the death rattle.

He stared up at the glowing face hovering before him. As he watched, the body below the face began to emerge from the darkness. To his surprise, Valentine noted that the dummy was clutching a Polaroid camera, raising it to eye-level in order to focus the lens on Valentine's face.

It was then that he found his voice at last. "Don't shoot!" he quavered. "Please don't shoot me!"

But the light exploded before Valentine's eyes. He sat up, blinking into sudden awareness.

The interior of the cabin presented its usual aspect—a mingling of white and shadow. There was no wall of darkness surrounding him, no incandescent image hovering over him, no camera aimed at his face.

Just a dream, he told himself, *but I could swear it was the light that woke me.*

Then, all at once, he saw the light again—as vivid and livid as he'd remembered. And now he knew its source.

Lightning. There, outside the window—

The plane began to buck violently and Valentine gripped the armrest. No doubt about it; the storm was getting worse.

He glanced down at his clutching hands, noting the whiteness of the knuckles. *Well, here we go again—back to square one*.

To hell with it. Perhaps the pills were working, or maybe he was just getting a little sense into his head at last; whatever the reason, he was damned if he'd let this storm spook him again. Pulling his fingers free from the armrest, Valentine reached over to the pouch-pocket at the base of the seat ahead and pulled out a copy of the airline's in-flight magazine. Switching on his overhead reading-light, he began to flick through the pages of the periodical.

The first thing that confronted him was a cigarette ad.

Valentine frowned. Much good *that* would do him now. Conscious of his need for nicotine, he ran the tip of his tongue over his dry upper lip and hastily turned the page to an article that bore a boldface heading—**Life Insurance And You.**

Sure, just what the doctor ordered. What the hell good were his cigarettes when he wasn't allowed to smoke them? And if this damned flying junk-heap crashed, there was no life insurance policy in the world big enough to cushion his fall.

Quickly he turned the page, only to find himself facing a telephone company advertisement. **Need Help? Use The Yellow Pages!**

Valentine scowled. Good advice, but no solution to his present problem. He was hardly in a position to pick up a phone, and even if he were able to do so, there were limits to the amount of aid he could expect. No operator would assist him in solving his problem, which, quite simply, was to find a way of getting off this plane alive.

Another sickening swoop shuddered through the aircraft, rattling the doors of the overhead compartments and sending the magazine sliding from his lap to the floor. As he stooped to retrieve it, a clap of thunder rose above the engine roar. Giving up, Valentine allowed his attention to wander to the window.

Squinting through his own reflection in the glass, he gazed out at the broad surface directly behind his seat-position. Through the murk, rain was pelting down on it in a torrent—each drop a dazzling diamond in the intermittent flicker of the beacon light at the wing's outer edge. The same series of flashes gave him a glimpse of the two big jet engines suspended by pods under the wing itself.

Again the thunder sounded and as it did so Valentine started to turn away. There was no point in staring out at the storm; he'd had his fill of it and needed no further reminder of its presence or the peril it presented. But then, out of the corner of his eye, he caught sight of something he hadn't noticed before. There was an extraneous object—a dark mass clinging to the far wing pod, just barely visible in the blink of the beacon light.

He thrust his face close to the glass again, cupping his hands to his eyes as he peered through his reflection into the clouded darkness and the driving rain. He saw—

Nothing.

Nothing there at all. It must have been his imagination—some momentary visual disturbance. Not too surprising, considering the content of his fears and the number of pills he'd swallowed to combat them. Unless, of course, he was hallucinating.

From the far recesses of his mind came the long-forgotten lyrics of a popular song he hadn't heard since he was a kid.

"I'm flying high—but I've got a feeling I'm falling—"

Valentine's scowl deepened as he felt the childhood fear welling up within him. He rubbed his eyes and glanced through the window once more, seeking final reassurance.

And there it was again—the dark distortion clinging to the engine pod!

Turning, he twisted his neck toward the window of the seat directly behind him, striving to get a better view.

As if to assist him, a vivid flash of lightning streaked across the sky. Its momentary glare gave him the better look he sought.

Better?

No, this was worse—far worse.

In the instant flicker of the lightning's greenish glare, he saw it all too clearly—the naked, apelike figure of a man, sitting astride the outboard engine!

Then the vision vanished in the darkness of the storm. Again the thunder rumbled.

And once more a jagged streak of green slashed through the sky. Valentine saw its source—the bolt of lightning issued from the creature's outstretched arms!

At the same moment, the aircraft yawed erratically, and the movement sent Valentine's head banging forward against the side of the window. For a split second his eyes closed involuntarily, responding to the impact. Forcing them open, he stared out once again. A flame of electrical current was streaming back across the wing. Straddling the outboard engine, the grotesque figure turned toward Valentine, its silvery face contorting in a grin.

"Oh my God!" Valentine flung himself back and his shout echoed through the confines of the cabin. "There's something outside! I saw it!"

If it was attention he wanted, his outcry brought immediate results.

As his fellow passengers peered perplexedly around the sides of the seats before him, the senior stewardess came rushing down the aisle.

Halting beside him, she glanced down solicitously.

"Something wrong?"

"Wrong?" Valentine forced the words out between chattering teeth. "Dear God in heaven! It's a man. There's a man out there on the wing!"

The staring circle of faces in the forward seats registered varying reactions of shock, puzzlement, and disbelief. The senior stewardess attempted a smile of reassurance. But from the seat behind him came the old lady's strident cackle.

"Yes, I see him—all green and slimy!" She cackled again. "It's my first husband!"

The old man seated beside her snorted in feigned disgust. "If it is, you drove him to it."

The stewardess moved briskly to the row behind Valentine's seat. Although she was standing beyond his range of vision, he could hear her voice quite clearly.

"Did you really see something out there?" she asked.

And now the old lady's voice: "Of course not. A man on the wing—what a howl!"

Another streak of greenish light exploded beyond Valentine's window. He pressed his face against the pane quickly, just before the flash faded into darkness; just long enough for its final flicker to reveal the surface of the wing and the twin engines mounted at its extremity. The figure had disappeared.

Staring out at the darkness, Valentine's eyes blinked in unison with the beacon lights. For a moment he stared at them in stunned silence, then turned to find the senior stewardess gazing down at him once again, a question in her eyes.

Valentine opened his mouth and the words came tumbling out. "There was lightning. At first I thought it was an animal out there—a dog or a cat. Then I realized it was a man. Maybe a technician trapped out there on takeoff." He shook his head. "My God, how could he survive? The air's too thin. The wind blast—so cold—and he's naked on top of it." Again he shook his head, sighing softly. "I know it's impossible."

The stewardess nodded sympathetically. Momentarily it occurred to Valentine that she might very probably just be humoring him, but right now any expression of concern was welcomed. Suddenly the younger stewardess appeared beside her companion and reached forward to extend the paper cup she held in her hand.

"Here you are," she said.

Valentine reached out for the cup and stared down suspiciously at its cloudy content. "What's this?"

The girl smiled. "Just some warm milk."

"You're sure there's nothing in it?"

The girl shook her head. But her companion produced the plastic pillbox from her jacket pocket. This time she didn't wait to ask his permission; unscrewing the cap, she shook two capsules into the palm of her hand and held them out to him.

"I really think you should take them now. They'll help."

Valentine hesitated, conscious that both stewardesses were staring at him expectantly; conscious too that passengers in the forward seats were watching and waiting. Valentine sensed what they were thinking. *Look at that flake back there. What do you think he's going to do next?*

The air in the cabin was cold, but Valentine felt the sudden warmth of his blush, the sudden moisture of tears welling up in his eyes.

Somehow he managed to smile. "Please forgive me," he murmured. "That was a damned-fool thing I pulled—"

At a loss for further words to cover his embarrassment, he swallowed the pills and washed them down with a sip of milk. Naturally he couldn't expect any instantaneous reaction from the medication, but somehow the mere act seemed to ease his tension. He glanced up at his guardian angels, shaking his head and chuckling softly. "Holy smoke, when I hallucinate it's a real production, isn't it? A naked man crawling along a 707 wing in a storm at thirty-five thousand feet. Can you imagine?"

With a smile of relief the senior stewardess reached up to open the compartment above his seat and pulled down a blanket. Unfolding it quickly, she tucked it around Valentine's waist as he took another sip of his milk. "Don't feel embarrassed," she told him. "Just try to relax and get a little sleep. We should be out of this disturbance soon."

"Thanks." Valentine settled back against the seat cushion and held out the empty cup. As she took it from him, he smiled again. "Funny, isn't it? The tricks your mind can play on you. How you can see things that don't exist."

But as he spoke, he was seeing something that very obviously *did* exist. Peering past the stewardess, he had a clear view of her junior companion standing at the end of the aisle before the open cockpit door of the plane, deep in conversation with a uniformed man who was probably the co-pilot. For a moment the man glanced in his direction, then nodded and turned to move back through the open entrance. As the door closed behind him, the younger stewardess disappeared into the galley.

Valentine focused his gaze on the face of the attendant hovering above him. "No need for you to stay," he said. "You must have other passengers to see to."

The senior stewardess shook her head. "I'd be happy to sit with you until you fall asleep."

The mother instinct. Valentine transformed his irritation into another smile. "Please, it would be easier if you weren't here."

"You're sure?"

"Positive. I'm drowsy already. Look—"

Eyes closing, he let his head drop forward in a semblance of slumber.

Peeking up, he saw her smile at his little joke and start to move away. As she did so he called after her softly, "Miss St. John—"

"Yes?" She turned, halting.

When he called, he really had no idea just what it was he intended to say, but suddenly he knew his purpose. He'd made a spectacle of himself back there but that was over with now. The important thing was to put an end to this mother-and-child relationship and reassert his status as a calm, mature, reasonable adult. Once he realized his role, his words came easily.

"You know, don't you, that should a plane crash, your chances of survival are significantly enhanced if you're in the back."

The senior stewardess nodded. "The plane won't crash, Mr. Valentine, but you're very kind to think of my welfare."

"That's okay," Valentine said. "I just wanted to make sure you knew. Good night."

SEGMENT 1 (JOHN LANDIS)

William Conner (Vic Morrow) steps out of his neighborhood tavern and into The Twilight Zone.

Conner is interrogated by two German officers (Remus Peets and Kai Wulff).

Conner, trapped on a ledge in occupied France, is used for target practice by the two German officers.

The first sight that William Conner has as he enters the second stage of his visit to The Twilight Zone.

The residents of Sunnyvale Rest Home are gathered for their weekly lecture on exercise and vitamins.

The rejected Mr. Conroy (Bill Quinn) once again heads back to his home away from home.

Mrs. Dempsey (Helen Shaw) reminisces about her youth.

Mr. Bloom (Scatman Crothers) entices Sunnyvale Rest Home's residents with stories of the magic of youth.

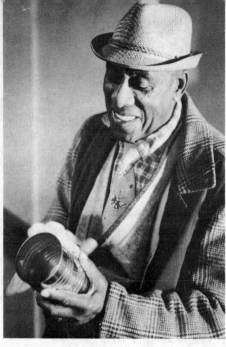

Mr. Bloom shines his magical can.

Mr. Bloom prepares the residents of Sunnyvale Rest Home for a game of "Kick the Can."

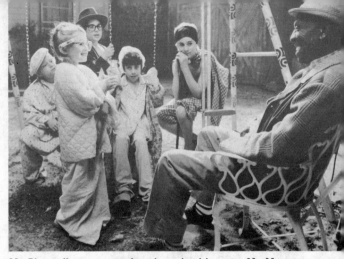

Mr. Bloom discusses new-found youth with young Mr. Mute (Christopher Eisenmann), young Mrs. Dempsey (Laura Mooney), young Mr. Weinstein (Scott Nemes), young Mrs. Weinstein (Tanya Fenmore) and young Mr. Agee (Evan Richards).

Mr. Conroy, Mrs. Dempsey and Mr. Weinstein (Martin Garner) look on as the young Mr. Agee escapes into The Twilight Zone.

Mr. Bloom departs Sunnyvale Rest Home to find other senior citizens with whom he can share his magic can.

SEGMENT 3 (JOE DANTE)

Helen Foley (Kathleen Quinlan) asks directions from the counterman (Dick Miller) at a wayside cafe.

Helen Foley checks on Anthony's (Jeremy Licht) bicycle.

Helen Foley and Anthony's Dad (William Schallert)

Anthony takes Helen upstairs to wash up.

Uncle Walt (Kevin McCarthy), Ethel (Nancy Cartwright), Anthony's mother (Patricia Barry) and Father try to figure out where dinner is.

Uncle Walt performs a hat trick for the family.

Helen and Anthony await the next surprise from Uncle Walt's hat.

Uncle Walt, Helen, Father and Mother look on in dread as they enter The Twilight Zone.

SEGMENT 4 (GEORGE MILLER)

The stewardesses, Diana (Abbe Lane) and Shelly (Donna Dixon), help Mr. Valentine (John Lithgow) to his seat.

A young passenger (Christina Nigra) reminds Mr. Valentine there is "No Smoking."

Mr. Valentine has embarked on a journey of fear into The Twilight Zone.

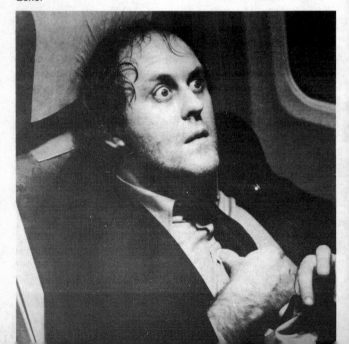

Valentine's frustration is about to cause a desperate act of self-preservation.

The Sky Marshall (Charles Knopf), Senior Stewardess, Junior Stewardess and the little girl look on as Valentine is subdued.

The Co-Pilot (John Dennis Johnston) attempts to quiet a frightened Mr. Valentine.

The Sky Marshall identifies himself to the Co-Pilot and offers help with the frightened passenger.

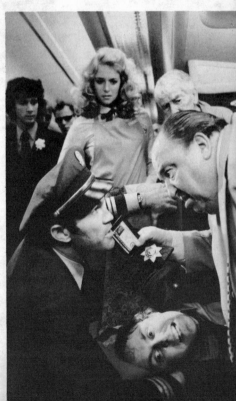

The Sky Marshall grabs hold of a desperate Valentine.

Mr. Valentine is loaded into a waiting ambulance.

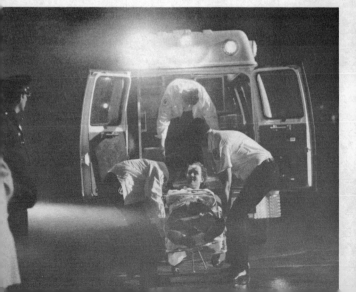

The trustworthy ground engineers (Frank Marshall and Jeffrey Lampert) are about to discover what ails Global Flight 44.

The passengers and crew of Flight 44 realize Valentine's story was not all imagination.

"Pleasant dreams."

Pleasant dreams?

Not for me, Valentine told himself. Definitely not for me at a time like this. A familiar quotation came to him. *"To sleep, perchance to dream; aye, there's the rub."*

Hamlet, wasn't it? Something of Shakespeare's that he knew. Great poet. Poor guy, he must have had his troubles too, if he came up with such a line. But he hadn't run into anything like this, that's for sure. Whatever his problems might have been, he'd lucked out.

Shakespeare never traveled by plane. Never got himself trapped in a freak storm. Never found himself buried in the bowels of a mechanical monster. Never sat helplessly suspended thirty-five thousand feet in midair, thirty-five thousand feet above the ground, wondering whether or not he'd touch down safely at the end of his journey instead of crashing in a fiery explosion.

"To be, or not to be; that is the question." Hamlet's question, Shakespeare's question, Valentine's question. But Hamlet was speaking rhetorically and Shakespeare was toying with an idea; Valentine alone faced a situation that was all too real. Hamlet spoke his lines and left the stage. Valentine was left to contemplate the problem with all its perilous possibilities. Alone, surrounded by storm-tossed sky, alone with his fears.

Sleep was the only avenue of escape. He settled back against his pillow. Might as well get some rest, give the medication a chance to work. How many of those capsules had he taken? Valentine couldn't remember; he only knew that he'd had more than enough. If he tried walking around now with all those pills inside him, he'd probably rattle.

But he wouldn't walk. And on second thought, he wouldn't sleep either—not if it meant running the risk of dreaming. Better to just rest, rest and relax, ride out the storm. No dreams, no more hallucinations.

Closing his eyes, he tried to close his mind as well. But the thought kept creeping in. *Hallucinations*. Could he be absolutely certain this was the answer?

According to the captain's intercom message at the beginning of the flight, the skies were clear.

But the storm had come, and it was real. Even in his present, pleasant state, fully drugged and half dozing, Valentine was vaguely conscious that the plane was still pitching, and a rumble of thunder still sounded faintly in his ears.

Yes, the storm was real. And if this was so, could he be absolutely sure that what he'd seen out there on the wing was purely a product of his imagination, a figment of fear?

Valentine searched his memory for a dictionary definition. *Figment*—something made up, fabricated, or contrived. But how could a mind capable of retaining a dictionary's definition also conjure up such a horrendous imaginary creation—a naked, manlike monstrosity riding on the wing through the stormy night like a witch straddling a broomstick?

There were no witches; that much Valentine

knew. And no one traveled by broomstick, even under clear skies.

But skies, clear or cloudy, serene or storm-beset, held strange secrets. Another memory crossed his mind, weaving in its wake a trailing tremor of terror.

The Bermuda Triangle.

How many times had he read about that vast mysterious expanse of ocean in which hundreds of ships had vanished without a trace over the centuries, in which thousands of voyagers had unaccountably disappeared forever?

And not just in the distant past, either; the phenomenon was still occurring today. Only now it wasn't just ships that disappeared. Within recent years their ranks had been swelled by countless numbers of aircraft that had taken off on routine flights, only to be lost in limbo. And not just single-passenger planes, either—among the missing were huge commercial flights. Even military missions had flown to their final fate somewhere in the vast expanse of sky above the Triangle.

Valentine vaguely recalled the strange story of a squadron—Navy, wasn't it?—that had set out from the Florida coast on a routine training exercise, only to disappear without warning following frantic radio signals that indicated that the pilots had somehow lost their bearings in the midst of strange cloud-formations suddenly surrounding them. When radio signals abruptly faded, a search party was dispatched—a larger aircraft, carrying a crew of fourteen. It too had vanished into empty air.

But *had* the air been empty?

Nobody knew. For that matter, there were still hundreds of thousands of square miles of the earth's surface; impenetrable jungles, desolate deserts, teeming jungles, mist-shrouded mountains, and forever-frozen polar wastes, which remained unexplored. And the oceans, roaring relentlessly over 70 percent of the globe, had still to yield their submerged secrets to the eyes of men.

Through the years, tens of thousands of sailing ships had made a safe passage through the Bermuda Triangle, tens of thousands had traversed the aerial routes above it without incident. But still the fact remained: so many ships had sunk into the sea's dank depths; so many planes had plunged into oblivion in the shrouded skies above.

And not in the Bermuda Triangle alone. There were many places where similar perils dwelt—travelers by sea or air had met an unknown fate in dozens of other localities scattered all around the globe. And scientists were still baffled by the presence of inexplicable phenomena in certain areas where compasses failed to function, natural causes produced unnatural results, and even the laws of gravity seemed suspended. What was it they'd come up with? Valentine seemed to recollect reading something about electromagnetic force-fields. A properly worded phrase, but one that explained nothing. Once, learned men believed that the air around and above them was filled with unseen presences. Today, they told us it was filled with unseen electrical disturbances. But no one really knew.

Some scientists still scoffed at the notion that the Bermuda Triangle and the air above it contained such forcefields, just as their academic ancestors had doubted the existence of demons.

But they had no proof. And while they argued, ships and planes and people continued to vanish on their voyages.

Valentine had a sudden image of a group of medieval theologians, hotly debating the question of how many angels could dance on the point of a pin. Then the vision was shockingly superseded by a phantasm of the grinning presence he'd glimpsed on the wing of the plane.

We didn't believe in such entities anymore, even though religion still retained them as realities. Strange, wasn't it? Despite the so-called advances of modern science, those religious beliefs still remain unchanged—beliefs in actual angelic presences and demonic dreads. Yet no man had even seen an angel, and no man had even seen a demon.

Except himself.

Valentine shuddered involuntarily as he sank further down in his seat. His eyes remained closed, but now the inner image rose before them once again—the insane image of the grinning, grotesque apparition astride the outboard engine on the wing, eyes flaming with a fire fueled in hell, its mouth gaping wide to reveal a forklike tongue darting forth from between the yellowed fangs. Now it began to crawl across the surface of the wing, inching its way toward him; then rising, it confronted him just beyond the window. Its clutching claws extended into cruel talons, ready to tear and rend, its fanged mouth opened wider in horrid hunger. In a moment it would spring forward, shattering the glass, its talons impaling him, tusks tearing his living flesh.

It was so close now that he could feel a belching blast of carrion breath, see the corded throat-muscles rise in rhythm with an ear-shattering roar of—

Thunder.

Valentine opened his eyes, realizing the source of the sound he'd heard; realizing too that what he had glimpsed was only the culmination of a nightmare.

But the thunder was real, and so was the throbbing of his heartbeat, half heard above the cabin clatter of the pitching plane.

He raised himself in his seat, turning to stare at the drawn window-blind. It *had* been a nightmare. The blind was closed, there was nothing beyond it; nothing out there at all except the storm. God, what a dream that had been!

But he was fully awake now, fully aware of his surroundings, and there was nothing to fear. Nothing to fear but fear itself. Nothing outside that window.

He turned away slowly to face the seat back directly before him. Perhaps if he closed his eyes again, sleep would return; a quiet peaceful sleep without dreams.

Valentine tried to lean back, tried to lower his lids again, but his eyes refused to close.

What was the matter with him now? Had he gone so far over the edge that he was even afraid of falling asleep?

That damned blind—

Valentine took a deep breath. Only one way to put an end to such nonsense. Forcing himself upright, he inhaled deeply once more. Then, leaning forward, he reached out, yanking up the blind.

And there, grinning at him through the window, was the face. The hideous mocking face of his nightmare.

Valentine screamed.

He jerked his head to one side, but not before catching a glimpse of the creature's upright hand. Clutched in its claws was a metallic object—a tangled cluster of steel fragments that looked as though they'd been torn from the plane's engine.

Valentine screamed again. As his head swiveled in the direction of the aisle, he saw them running toward him—the junior stewardess, the fat man from the forward seat, the uniformed copilot.

Valentine fragmented his scream into words.

"It's out there. It's real!" He began to sob hysterically. "My God! What's happening to me?"

Then they were upon him, pinning him against his seat. Staring past the circle of troubled faces he caught a glimpse of the little girl standing in the aisle behind them. She was holding something before her face and for an instant her features were obscured by a flash of light. Then Valentine realized what was happening. The little bitch had taken his picture!

Impulsively he struggled to rise. Hands darted out from the circle around him, pushing him down. The copilot turned his head, shouting an order that Valentine was unable to hear above the roar of the engine.

Gasping, Valentine managed to free his right arm, but only for a moment. Just long enough to stab his forefinger in the direction of the window.

"There it is!" he shouted. "Look—"

They *were* looking now and as they did so, their expressions changed. Valentine stared up, searching their faces for a reaction he did not find. And when they turned back to him, there was no horror in their eyes; only pity.

Somehow that was even harder for him to bear than horror. Still sobbing, he forced his gaze toward the window. Beyond the rectangular pane there was only darkness.

The face had disappeared.

Crazy. I'm going mad, he told himself. But they were all crazy, all these nice, normal people who were holding him down as if he were some kind of wild animal, ready to spring at their throats. And as the fat man eased off from his kneeling position on the armrest beside him, Valentine noted something that was crazier still. Just before the bunched-up trouser leg slid back down to cover the man's bulging calf, Valentine saw that he was wearing a gun strapped to his ankle. Valentine blinked. *Jesus, what gives here? Don't tell me I'm hallucinating again.*

A moment later the explanation came as the fat

man turned to the copilot and pulled a wallet from his jacket pocket. Opening it, he exhibited a badge.

"Sky marshal, eh?" The copilot nodded. "Good thing you're here."

Valentine relaxed momentarily. At least the presence of the gun was explained now; its reality assured him he wasn't *that* crazy.

Now the senior stewardess was coming down the aisle. As she moved toward the group, he noted that she was holding her right hand behind her back. Valentine groaned inwardly. Good God, was she going to feed him more pills?

As she approached, the copilot turned to glance at the passengers clustering concernedly in the aisle behind him. He spoke with quiet authority.

"I want you all to please return to your seats. I'd like a word alone with Mr. Valentine."

He nodded at the younger stewardess. She moved beyond the range of Valentine's vision, herding the curious onlookers toward the rear of the plane. But the little girl still stood behind the senior stewardess, and now she stared down at what was concealed behind Miss St. John's back, her eyes widening.

"Handcuffs!" she exclaimed. "Far out!"

Valentine glanced up in shock as the senior stewardess brought her right hand forward, abandoning any further attempt at concealment. The steel cuffs dangled before him, glittering under the light of the reading lamp, but his eyes never left her face. She reddened before his accusing gaze, her expression conveying a mixture of contrition and concern.

Across the aisle, the fat sky marshal sank into the

seat formerly occupied by the little girl. Miraculously, the child's mother had managed to remain asleep through all the confusion, but now she awoke and stared with blinking eyes at the handcuffs, which the senior stewardess was holding, then at the little girl standing beside her. She nudged the fat man as she spoke. "Don't tell me they're going to put those things on my kid! What has she done this time!"

The fat man turned to her and began to whisper an explanation. Then Valentine lost sight of the duo as the copilot reached over him and gently slid the window-blind down.

"Now then," he said softly. "What seems to be the problem?"

"Nothing at all," Valentine told him. "I'm sorry I shouted."

For a moment he hesitated, wondering whether or not the copilot could be trusted with the truth. Then his eyes strayed to the handcuffs, which the senior stewardess held before her, and the answer came quickly. He couldn't trust them and they certainly weren't trusting him. No sense trying to tell the truth; obviously they wouldn't believe him. He'd have to play it their way. "I had a nightmare," he said.

The copilot nodded. "I'm aware of that, Mr. Valentine. But you've got to understand my position. This plane is flying in a severe storm. There's no immediate danger, but frankly we've got our hands full up front as it is. Now I have a passenger acting irrationally, threatening the safety of my aircraft. That leaves me with two choices. If there is no further disturbance, I can ignore the problem. Or else I can ask the sky marshal over there to apply these handcuffs." He paused, letting the message sink in. "What would you do, Mr. Valentine?"

Valentine hesitated before replying. He scanned the faces before him, reading the question in the copilot's eyes, the senior stewardess's concern, the little girl's gleeful excitement. No, he couldn't afford to tell the truth—not the whole truth, anyway. But somehow he had to impress them with their peril. Taking a deep breath, he spoke quickly.

"I'll level with you. Being suspended up here at thirty-five thousand feet in the middle of a storm, with no visible means of support, scares the hell out of me." He took another deep breath, then continued. "On the other hand, reason tells me I'm perfectly safe. Under normal circumstances we ought to get through this all in one piece. Trouble is, these circumstances are not normal. You know it and I know it. We're in trouble. And if we ignore that fact, we're all going to die—"

"What fact?" The copilot frowned. "What exactly are you saying?"

"There's something wrong with one of your engines."

The copilot's frown deepened. "What do you mean?"

"It is not working," Valentine said.

"Which engine?"

Valentine met his stare. "Outboard number one."

The copilot and the senior stewardess exchanged

troubled glances, and then the uniformed man bent over Valentine, speaking softly. "How could you know that?"

Valentine shrugged. "I just know it," he said. "Don't ask me how."

Now it was the copilot's turn to take a deep breath. "All right, Mr. Valentine. Maybe you had a hunch, or maybe you just made a lucky guess, but it's true. Nine minutes ago, engine number one was struck by lightning. There was a flame-out. The point is, we still have three engines functioning perfectly. There's no reason to alarm the other passengers and no reason to alarm yourself. Take my word for it—we're perfectly capable of remaining airborne under our present power without any further problems." He glanced down at his watch. "I estimate we'll touch down in twenty minutes."

So that's that, Valentine told himself. At least they'd got the message and maybe there'd be no more trouble now; all he could do was hope that the flight crew did their job. If he said any more, it would only make matters worse. He glanced up at the copilot and smiled. "Thanks for the explanation. What you say makes sense, of course, and I promise I won't trouble you any further."

As the copilot nodded, the aircraft pitched violently. For a moment Valentine lost his cool. "Go fly the plane!" he cried.

The voice of the old lady rose from the seat behind him. "Good idea! We'll behave ourselves, won't we, sonny?"

Once more the copilot glanced at the senior

stewardess, then turned and started down the aisle. As he disappeared from view, the senior stewardess leaned forward. "Don't worry, Mr. Valentine. You heard what he said—we'll be on the tarmac in twenty minutes."

But her words were punctuated by a loud bang as the plane bucked again and the overhead compartment flew open. She reached up to close it, but another violent lurch toppled her backward across the aisle and into the lap of the sky marshal.

Almost simultaneously, three more overhead lockers burst open. The door of a closet opposite the galley suddenly swung forward. An oxygen cylinder toppled out and began to roll down the aisle.

With each convulsive movement of the plane came an accompaniment of terrifying sound—a combination of structural stress and engine protest that resonated through the confines of the cabin. Over the violent vibration, the murmur of frightened passengers arose.

Leaning forward, Valentine peered along the aisle. Nobody was watching him now. The young couple up ahead were clinging to each other like frightened monkeys swaying in a storm-swept treetop. The fat man was clutching the armrest, his eyes closed, jowls quivering. The little girl in the seat before him gripped her precious Polaroid tightly. Valentine couldn't see her face, nor that of the elderly woman seated behind him, but he heard her clearly as she addressed the old man beside her:

"This is not very amusing!"

"What do you mean?" her husband replied. "It's a million laughs! Haven't you ever been on a roller coaster before?"

Valentine wasn't laughing. And this wasn't a roller coaster ride. It wasn't just turbulence either —something besides the storm was responsible for such rapid pitching and yawing—the sensation was so intense that it felt as if the entire plane was being ripped and shaken by some gigantic hand. Something else was at work out there, some maniacal force—

Impulsively, he reached out and jerked up the window-blind. Staring past his reflection, staring through the rushing rain streaming over the wing, staring through the inky darkness punctuated by the flicker of the beacon light, he saw it again.

The naked man—the ape, the creature—was crouching at the far end and rocking the wing flaps back and forth. Valentine's eyes widened in shock as the creature turned to acknowledge his presence with a ghastly grin. Valentine jerked his head away, seeking reassurance in reality.

But as his eyes scanned the confines of the cabin, he found no comfort. Fighting to maintain balance in the midst of momentum of motion, the young couple still clung to one another; the little girl gripped her camera in one hand and clung to her armrest with the other as she bounced in rhythm to every pitch and plunge. Across the aisle, the sky marshal hunched forward with lowered head, ashen lips moving as he twisted the beads in his hand, reciting the rosary.

Stifling an impulse to scream, Valentine turned to stare out the window once again. What he saw stunned him into silence.

The silver-skinned creature was sitting astride the inboard engine, its claws ripping off the cowling!

No use trying to scream now; Valentine's throat muscles were contracted with terror.

As the cowling tore loose, the creature dipped one clawlike hand into the opening, pulling out bits and pieces of the engine and tossing them over his shoulder.

Valentine shuddered convulsively, trying to avert his gaze, but his paralyzed muscles refused to respond.

Now, incredibly, the apparition squatting on the wing was tearing loose a fuel line. Oil gushed forth, spraying like water from a garden hose. As Valentine watched, the creature bent forward, encircling the loose end with greedy lips.

My God, he's drinking from it!

Summoning all his strength, Valentine heaved backward and turned to face the cabin's interior once more.

Here another shock awaited him. The little girl stood in the aisle beside him, swaying to maintain her balance and aiming her Polaroid toward his face.

"No you don't!" Valentine cried. "Give it to me!" His hand lunged out, tugging the camera from her grasp. Then he turned to the window, raising the Polaroid and squinting through the view-finder until it focused on the figure beyond the pane. The camera clicked; lowering it, he tore the strip of exposed film free and held it up, waiting for the photo to develop.

"Hey, turkey! Gimme that back!" The child grabbed at the camera in his other hand and Valentine made no resistance. As she moved away he sat in agonized impatience, watching the image emerge on the film. Gradually a shadowy shape appeared, still blurred and indistinguishable.

The plane lurched sharply. Holding the print between his fingers, Valentine jerked around in his seat to peer through the window once more.

The creature had changed position. For a moment Valentine was conscious of a bulge between its shoulder blades as though the thing had a hump on its back. But there was no time to discern it clearly; all he could do was stare as the creature leaned over the leading edge of the engine pod. It was throwing fragments of the engine into the turbine intake!

The engine screamed its protest through the night. The creature looked up at Valentine with its mocking grin, then dropped more metal fragments into the intake. The plane thrashed violently.

Valentine let the photo fall from his hand. To hell with the picture—if that creature out there wasn't stopped, another engine would be destroyed and then—

Something bumped against the base of Valentine's seat. Glancing down, he saw the oxygen cylinder rolling in the aisle below. Scooping it up he lunged at the window, smashing at the Plexiglas. As he did so, he found his voice and raised it in a shout.

"It's real, there's a thing out there—!"

The sky marshal dived across the aisle, dragging him away from the window. As they fell back, Valentine let the oxygen cylinder drop. For a moment the two men struggled, but the fat man's weight was no match for the strength born of Valentine's fear. Desperately, he freed his right hand and reached down to yank the hand gun from the sky marshal's ankle holster. Wrenching free, he aimed the weapon at the window and fired.

There was a shatter of glass—then the irresistible rush of air as the cabin decompressed. Magazines, plastic cups, and table napkins whirled wildly. Oxygen masks dropped from the ceiling, dangling and twisting like suspended serpents.

The force of the implosion sucked Valentine halfway through the window and the fat man grabbed his legs, hanging on for dear life. Icy wind ripped across his face, filling his nostrils with frozen fire and half blinding him with its fury.

In the aisle behind them the senior stewardess staggered and fell; plates and silverware poured forth from the galley shelves. Amidst screams and shouts drowned by the sound of the wind, a thump echoed as the overhead projecter module dropped down from the ceiling and the inflight movie started up on its own accord. As the movie screen swung back and forth in the gusting wind, the studio logo flickered on.

Valentine saw none of this. Still protruding halfway from the window, thrashing about against the horrendous wind-blast as the fat man frantically clutched his legs, he stared out at the creature on the wing.

Now it turned, grinning again.

Dear God, it's coming after me!

Summoning his last ounce of strength, Valentine raised the hand gun still clutched between his fingers and fired.

The bullet found its mark in the creature's stomach. Casually, the thing reached down and plucked the missile off his hide the way one would remove some annoying insect. Raising the bullet to his gaping mouth, he *swallowed* it.

Then he advanced along the wing toward Valentine.

Valentine squeezed the trigger again . . . and again . . .

The creature's claws rose with blinding speed, picking the bullets out of the air like flies, gulping them down as he moved nearer.

Ultimately, Valentine's finger kept pressing the trigger, even after he realized the bullets were spent.

Now, as he looked up, the grinning face loomed before him. One claw darted out and Valentine felt the cruel talons close around his wrist. Then it released its grip and grabbed the gun.

Raising the weapon to its mouth the creature began to chomp on the barrel, chewing it up bit by bit like a child eating a candy bar.

At that moment a bright light burst from somewhere below, flaring up into its face.

The creature glanced down quickly and Valentine followed its gaze.

Below him he saw the landing lights of the airport-runway beacons blazing through the clear air beneath the cloudbank.

The silvery thing turned back again, frowning for a moment, its arms extended. Valentine, wedged in the window, waited his final fate.

Then, as the lights grew stronger, the monstrosity glanced at him once more. For a moment, Valentine could have sworn it winked at him, its outstretched claw waggling in a playful gesture.

Playful? Had it merely been *playing* all along? Now it turned and Valentine watched as the hump-like mass between its shoulder blades suddenly extended and expanded into webbed wings. The creature moved back, its wings spreading wide, then plunged forward and soared off into the night.

That was when Valentine fainted.

He was still unconscious when the wheels of the aircraft touched the glistening tarmac. He didn't see the passengers or hear their excited interchange as they stumbled down the steps and straggled across to the terminal gates. He wasn't aware of being pulled back to safety in the cabin as the plane made its descent, nor did he awaken when the ambulance crew arrived to bring him out of the cabin and wheel him into the waiting ambulance below.

He never saw the fully developed Polaroid he'd taken and perhaps that was just as well.

It was the senior stewardess who picked it up eventually from the debris-strewn cabin floor and stared down at the image—the image of Valentine. He had taken a photo of his own reflection.

Nor did Valentine see the mangled, smoking engines as the ground crew clustered around them. One of the mechanics approached with a scowl. "Hey—what the hell gives?"

Then he and the others stepped back hastily. There was a shrill grating sound as the inboard pod gave way, and the engine dropped onto the tarmac with a crash.

The scowling mechanic shook his head, then raised his eyes to ask the final question: *"Holy Christ—what happened up there?"*

There was no answer. The skies above were clear in the gathering twilight.

Or were they. . . .?

3

HELEN

The lights in the room were just a little too dim for proper vision, but Mama didn't care. The music was a trifle soft for anyone who might be a bit hard of hearing, but Mama didn't care about that either. Most people disliked being stared at by strangers, but this didn't bother Mama at all.

Because Mama was dead.

Mama was dead, and nothing in the world would

ever bother her again. She wasn't concerned about the clumsy fashion in which the mortician had arranged her hair or about his overzealous application of makeup to her sunken cheeks. As a matter of fact, her cheeks weren't sunken anymore; they had been carefully filled out with cotton stuffed inside her mouth, and two little wires were placed just inside the corners of her lips, fixing them in a permanently peaceful smile.

Mama was not disturbed by the sickly scent of floral bouquets already wilting in the heat of the stuffy Slumber Room. She wasn't worried about the cost of the overpriced casket in which she rested, nor was she wondering just how it would be paid for.

Mama's troubles were over, and for a moment Helen almost envied her.

No more problems, no more tears; these were for the living. Standing beside the open casket, Helen Foley glanced up at her sister Vivian.

It was Vivian who shed the tears. And as usual, Helen was left to confront the problems.

It had always been that way, ever since Helen could remember. Vivian was the beauty of the family, the little charmer, and when her pretty face was marred by teardrops, Mama did everything in her power to comfort the poor darling and make her happy again. Helen wasn't really homely, but she lacked her sister's charisma.

"Looks aren't everything," Mama used to say. "Maybe you're not exactly beautiful, but you've got a good brain. Just use it and everything will be all right. You'll see."

So Vivian smiled and pouted her way through life, short on skills but relying on long eyelashes and ample cleavage to win her permanent security—a loyal and loving husband, two adorable children, a good home, and a circle of admiring friends.

Helen took Mama's advice to heart. She used her brains, studied hard. Vivian had been the Prom Queen but it was Helen who graduated at the head of the class and went on to a teaching career.

And here she was, ten years later; with any luck she could contine teaching right up until the day when she would join Mama forever in the family plot at Rose Hill Cemetery. So much for brains and Mama's counsel.

For a moment Helen gazed down at her mother's face, feeling the old anger rise within her. Then she sighed softly.

No sense resenting Mama's advice; it was she herself who was to be blamed for taking it, and it was too late to change matters now. Vivian would continue to cry to be comforted, poor little thing; Helen would go on coping, facing each problem as it arose and solving all of them except her own.

Last week, when Mama died after the operation, Vivian had hysterics and took to her bed, surrounded by her family and comforted by their concern. It was Helen who had to come running to the rescue, go through the grim business of filling out the forms, making the funeral arrangements, handling details and down payments. After all, isn't that what brains are for?

Helen sighed again. Mama couldn't help her now, but neither could self-pity. No sense dwelling on the past; it was time to think of the future and she had already made up her mind.

Vivian glanced up, her sobs subsiding. "I suppose you'll be leaving," she said.

Helen nodded. "Right after the funeral. No reason to stay, now that Mama's gone."

"You really mean that, don't you?" Vivian seemed perplexed, rather than concerned. "What about your job?"

"It doesn't matter. I don't even feel like a teacher anymore. I've got nothing left to give those kids that means anything."

Helen answered without premeditation, but as she spoke she realized the truth of her words. "I'm running on empty, Viv. I've got to make the break now. I stayed in town as long as Mama needed me, but I can't go on here in the same old rut forever. I feel all used up inside."

"I know what you mean," Vivian said. But from the way her mouth tightened, Helen knew she didn't understand. "It's just that you don't seem to realize you'll be leaving your whole life behind you."

Helen nodded. "I do realize it." She paused. "That's exactly the reason I'm going."

Vivian stared at her in concern. Self-concern, of course; it was the only kind she knew. "But if you go, what about me?"

"You have your own life—Jim and the kids. That's not what I thought I wanted, remember?"

"I remember." Vivian dabbed at her eyes with a handkerchief. "So what is it you think you want now?"

"I wish I knew."

Helen hesitated for a moment, listening to the soft strings of the piped-in organ music, the familiar melody that seemed to haunt the halls of every funeral parlor. She and Vivian had probably heard it a hundred times before and the way each of them identified it probably defined the difference between them. Vivian knew the melody simply as a song "Going Home." Helen recognized it as the Largo from Dvorak's *New World*. To be more precise, his Ninth Symphony in E, Opus Ninety-Five. Yes, that was the real difference between the two of them. All those years of learning left her a single legacy—a brain full of trivia, which nobody, including grubby students, cared about, while empty-headed Vivian ended up with everything she'd always wanted, everything she needed for the good life as it was lived in suburbia.

"Sorry, Viv," she said. "I guess I'm not sure myself about what I really want. But I know it's not here, not in Homewood. Not for me."

"Well, if you've made up your mind—" Vivian shrugged, her voice softening. "I just thought maybe I could talk you out of it."

Helen shook her head. "Not this time."

"I only hope you know where you're going." Vivian sighed again, then brightened. "Listen to what they're playing," she said. "I always liked that piece. What did they call it?" She smiled. "Oh, I remember now—it's 'Going Home.' "

So that was that.

Once the funeral ended, everybody was going home; Vivian to her family, Mama to heaven, granted there was such a place to go. And now Helen was alone. Only she and Thomas Wolfe seemed to realize that you can't go home again.

She drove along in the afternoon sunlight, music blaring from her car radio. Punk rock, of course; Dvorak was strictly for funeral parlors nowadays. "Slumber Room"—how she hated the hypocritical euphemism! But maybe that was the correct designation for one of the few places left in the world where one could take refuge in the soothing solace of sleep, undisturbed by the ceaseless clamor of savage sound. What kind of sacred music would they be playing when today's children were laid to rest? "Punk Rock of Ages, Cleft for Me?"

Helen leaned forward, switching off the music. Hearing it only evoked an unpleasant recollection of the life she fled from; memories of classrooms filled with rebellious youngsters moving to the beat of a different drum, the twang of guitars, the screech of voices raised in dissonant defiance.

They were all alike today, or so it seemed; underprivileged kids from broken families that gave them too little and overprivileged kids from broken families that gave them too much. But like herself, they seemed to have found no home to go to, and so they dropped out, tripped out, freaked out into an artificial existence of chemically induced sensation, surrounding themselves with a protective barrier of stereophonic sound.

Helen shook her head ruefully. No sense going overboard; the least she could do was to own up to the truth. Not all youngsters were on drugs, not all of them flouted authority. But even the conformists seemed to be hooked on sound, ODing on decibels. They sought noise everywhere; injecting their eardrums with a daily dosage of rock, mainlining on the shrieks and groans of splatter-films, the cacophony of commercial commands from their television sets, the clatter of clamor of video-games. No wonder the voices of parents and teachers alike were lost in the din. Teaching was an art, and like all arts it depended upon communication. But how can you hope to communicate with anyone in the midst of all that noise?

Maybe that's what she was really running from. Running from the noise that negated every effort to fulfill the life she'd chosen. What was the sense of trying to teach when nobody *listened?*

Helen shook her head. Big deal! It was easy enough to see the problems; the hard part was to come up with the proper solutions. She knew the questions, all right, but not the answers. And when you don't have any answers, what is there left for you to teach?

That was the bottom line. She wasn't running away from noise, youthful protests, or social upheaval. She was running, and running scared, from the realization of her ignorance.

I don't want to be a teacher anymore, she told herself. *I want to be a learner.*

Abruptly she glanced up at a roadside sign on the right, noting its message. CLIFFORDSVILLE 5.

Cliffordsville? Helen glanced at her watch quickly. Almost five o'clock—she should have been in Willoughby at least half an hour ago at the rate she was traveling. What was she doing five miles away from a town she hadn't even noticed on the roadmap? And why hadn't she had the sense to bring the map along with her?

She shook her head. All this worrying about kids who don't pay attention, and where does it get you? Lost, that's where. *If I really want to be a learner, I'd better start right now.*

Peering through the windshield against the slanting rays of midafternoon sun, Helen saw the outline of a small structure set back from the highway ahead and to her left.

As she neared it, she noted the lettered injunction of the sign mounted atop its flat roof—*Eat*.

Helen had private reservations about the wisdom of obeying such a command; her past experience with roadside cafes in godforsaken rural areas like this had not been all that pleasant. Nevertheless, she swerved to the left and entered the parking area before the weatherbeaten structure. There were only two other cars parked beside the entrance and she pulled up a short distance away. Then she moved across the gravel to the door.

As she opened it, a wave of warm air fanned her face, carrying with it the all-too-familiar reek of fast-food at its greasiest—a stomach-churning composite of French fries, cheeseburgers, and frozen pizzas which had been subjected to ordeal by fire.

Thank heaven she'd had a late breakfast before taking off! As it was she could make do with a cup of coffee; it was probably the only thing she could order here that wasn't fried. What she was really looking for, of course, was a roadmap.

Luck was with her. Seating herself on a counter stool, Helen confronted a multitalented, middle-aged man serving as the maitre d', chef, waiter, and busboy.

"What'll it be, miss?" he asked.

Helen told him what it would be, and as he busied himself at the coffee urn, she glanced past the side of the counter toward the two men seated at a corner table. Both appeared to be in their mid-thirties, too old for playing but happily resigned to their role as full-time spectators and sports commentators.

Glancing over their beer, they stared raptly at the screen of the television set mounted above the counter at the far end.

Jocks tossed a football across the full length of the nineteen-inch tube, then tumbled in a writhing heap at its base, their minuscule movements accompanied by the excited outcries of an unseen sportscaster.

More noise. Helen shrugged; no matter where you went, you couldn't get away from it.

Then, glancing down the counter in the opposite direction, she discovered another source of sound —the electronic emanation from a video-game enthusiastically operated by a small boy. At first glance he didn't appear to be any older than ten; if so, why wasn't he in school at this hour?

Helen frowned at the thought. *There you go again, still playing teacher! I thought we were through with all that, remember?*

Her frown vanished as the counterman set the coffee mug before her.

"Would that be all?" he asked. A pudgy thumb gestured toward the flyspecked glass container on the shelf directly behind him. "We got some nice pie, just came in today."

Helen shook her head. "You know what I want for dessert?" she said. "A nice, fresh roadmap."

The counterman's forehead furrowed into a frown and Helen nodded quickly. "Really—if you have one, I'd be very much obliged if you'd let me take a look at it."

The counterman's face relaxed in an amiable grin. "Sure thing. Got one lying around someplace —think I stuck it under the register."

Helen sipped her coffee as he moved away. In a moment he returned, brandishing the highway map triumphantly.

"Here you are."

He placed his find on the countertop before her. Helen lifted it gingerly. It was a map, no doubt about that, but one could hardly call it fresh. The outer surface was wrinkled and creased; and when she unfolded it, she was confronted with smudges of grease, which streaked and stained most of this area and the surrounding counties. Whoever fried this map hadn't done a very good job, Helen decided. But if she wanted to see what's cooking—

Helen studied the map for a moment, eyes narrowing as she squinted through the stains, then halted with a sigh of exasperation. "Okay, I give up. Where am I?"

The counterman jabbed a greasy forefinger at a smudge in the center of the map. "Here. You want the main highway, right?"

Helen nodded. "I guess so."

The counterman's finger moved a trifle to the left. "Looks like you missed the turnoff at Cliffordsville."

"Oh—I see."

Mine host smiled knowingly; he was in his glory now. "Look—about two miles back, you come to a gas station. That's Cayuga. You hang a left, go four blocks, and the highway cuts across. There you—"

He broke off as banging sounds rose from the far corner.

Helen turned and saw the source of the disturbance. The kid was pounding the side of the video-game, and each blow caused a blip of interference on the TV picture, much to the annoyance of the two customers watching the game.

Raising his voice over the noise of repeated banging, the counterman called out, "Hey, kid, easy on the machinery!"

The blows ceased abruptly as the boy glanced up. "It doesn't work right," he said.

The counterman shrugged. "Look, kid, I don't build the games, I just keep the quarters. Put in another one. Maybe it'll work better."

He turned back to Helen and his finger moved down to the map again. "See, just outside Cayuga, the highway splits off—"

A sudden series of thumps echoed through the confines of the cafe and he broke off, frowning.

One of the men at the table called loudly. "Hey, Walter, the kid's screwing up the TV!"

The counterman shrugged. "It's his quarter. The TV's free."

The other customer shared his companion's scowl. "To hell with that noise! I got twenty bucks riding on this game!"

The counterman nodded toward the youngster standing in front of the video-game. "You heard the man," he said. "Let's cool it, huh?"

The boy didn't reply. Inserting another quarter, he resumed his play, this time without a pounding accompaniment.

Now the only counterpoint to the counterman's conversation came from the continuing babble of the TV sportscaster.

As Helen watched, her informant began to fold the map as carefully as if the grease-spattered chart contained clues to the location of buried treasure. "You say you're headed for Willoughby?"

"That's right." Helen nodded.

"Nice town. You got a job set up there, or what?"

"Not really. I thought I'd just take a look around."

The counterman placed the folded map in his

right-hand trouser pocket with tender loving care. "Where're you from?" he asked.

"Homewood. That's downstate."

"I know the place." He nodded. "Nice town."

Helen smiled. "If you say so."

Over the continuing chatter of commentary issuing from the television came the sound of a phone ringing from the galley behind the counter. The proprietor turned and headed for it, leaving Helen to finish her coffee in peace.

But not for long.

From the television set the commentator's voice rose in crescendo, heralding a climactic crisis in the final moments of the last quarter. Then it faded abruptly at the sound of repeated bangings. Helen swung around on her stool to watch the youngster belaboring the side of the video-game machine with the flat of his hands.

Overhead, the TV picture scrambled completely. One of the men at the table groaned and his companion turned to glare at the instigator of the interruption.

"Cut out that goddam pounding!" he shouted. "You hear me?"

Ignoring him, the boy concentrated on the video-screen before him, then smacked the side of the machine again.

Helen stared uneasily, fumbling in her purse for change. All she wanted now was to get out of here before trouble started.

But it had already begun.

One of the men at the table pushed back his chair

and rose quickly. It wasn't until he stood up that Helen realized how big he was; over six feet tall, burly and broad-shouldered.

His companion looked up, gesturing. "Hey, Charlie, take it easy—"

Charlie wasn't listening. He headed toward the video-game in a cold rage, grabbing the boy by the shoulder and shoving him roughly to one side. Then he stooped and ripped the plug of the machine from the wall. Caught off balance, the youngster stumbled and fell against the baseboard.

Almost before she realized it, Helen was on her feet. "Stop that!" she cried.

Suddenly there was silence, all eyes focussing on Helen as she moved to the far wall and helped the child to his feet.

As she did so, their eyes met briefly. To her surprise, Helen saw that the boy was smiling. Turning abruptly, he ran to the door, yanked it open, and raced out.

Embarrassed, the big man lowered his gaze, then moved away to resume his seat at the table.

Helen glanced toward the counter; behind it, the counterman stood staring, and his worried expression told her he'd returned in time to witness the altercation.

"Sorry, lady," he murmured. "These guys—they take their sports real serious."

Helen nodded. "Nice town."

Moving to the door she made her exit, letting it slam behind her.

Only then did she relax. *Peace.*

Crossing to her car, she shook her head in rueful self-reproval. Why had she allowed herself to lose her temper that way? What happened back there was really none of her business; but on the other hand, she had no choice. She just couldn't stand to see a child mistreated that way. Thank God he hadn't been hurt.

Reaching the car, Helen slid her key into the door lock, glancing around as she did so. The parking area was deserted; the boy had disappeared.

Probably ran all the way home, Helen decided. And yet he hadn't seemed frightened.

Helen remembered the way he'd smiled when she'd helped him to his feet. There was something odd about that smile; was she imagining things, or had it conveyed a hint of secret understanding? Funny kid.

Funny Helen. Sliding into the seat before the steering wheel, she shook her head, remembering her resolution. Time to forget about what had happened, time to put the show on the road and make it over to Willoughby before dark.

Closing the door, she glanced through the side window, noting with surprise that twilight had already descended. To emphasize its coming, a neon beer-sign blinked on above the cafe entrance.

Helen turned the key in the ignition and the motor started. As her foot found the gas pedal, she released her parking brake, put the car in reverse, and started to back out before turning toward the driveway exit.

Suddenly she glanced up at the rearview mirror just in time to see a blur of movement behind her. Through the twilight she caught a glimpse of the boy on a bicycle speeding directly across the lot behind her.

Quickly she floored the brake, but as the car screeched to a halt there was a sudden, sickening thud.

"Oh my God!" she cried.

Wrenching the door open, Helen lunged out and headed around the side of the car at a dead run. Then she halted behind it, staring down in shock.

The boy was sprawled on the pavement beside his bike, eyes closed, breathing hard. Then, as she bent over him, his eyes opened.

"Are you all right?" Helen gasped.

The child nodded. "Yeah—I guess so—"

Helen knelt beside him. "Can you move your arms and legs?"

"Uh huh."

As Helen watched anxiously, the youngster started to sit up.

"Easy there," she said. "Tell me where it hurts."

They boy rubbed his left shoulder. "Just here. I must've hit it when I fell off." He smiled, shaking his head. "Don't worry, it's not broke or anything."

He started to get up and Helen put her hand on his arm, slowing his movement. "Not too fast," she said. "See if you can put your weight on your feet."

"Sure—you see?" The boy stood erect, rubbing his shoulder. "It doesn't hurt anymore, honest."

Now, for the first time, Helen turned her

attention to the bike. Its wheels lay bent and twisted beneath the rear tires of the car. The boy followed her stare, his smile of reassurance fading.

"Oh, I'm so sorry!" Helen turned to the youngster, speaking quickly. "Look, maybe you can get it fixed. I'll pay for it—"

"That's okay." The youngster's smile returned for a moment, then disappeared once more as he peered uncertainly around the dusk-dimmed parking area. "Do you think maybe you could give me a lift home? Before it gets dark?"

"Of course." Helen nodded, then glanced at her car trunk frowning. "I'm afraid there's no room for your bike, though. I'm moving and the backseat is loaded. The rest of my things are in the trunk."

"I can get it tomorrow." The boy bent down, tugging the bike free from beneath the tire, then dragged it across the lot and leaned it up against the wall of the cafe.

"You're sure it'll be safe there?" Helen said.

"Yeah. No sweat." The youngster returned, moving around the side of the car to the passenger door. He waited while Helen slid into the driver's seat and leaned over to unlock the door, then pushed it open so that he could enter.

As he settled down beside her, closing the door, she released the brake and started up the motor again. The car moved forward to the edge of the road. There it halted as Helen glanced at her passenger.

"Which way?" she asked.

"Make a left." The youngster nodded up at her. "The same way you're going."

Helen blinked. "How do you know which way I'm going?"

"I heard you talking back there."

"Did you now? You've got good ears."

The car picked up speed, moving down the road in the gathering twilight. There was no traffic and as Helen switched on her headlights, their glow seemed to emphasize the darkness of the lonely countryside ahead.

She peered through the windshield, waiting to catch a glimpse of the filling station that the counterman had mentioned, but now she felt the boy's hand nudge her arm.

"Turn here," he said, indicating a side road branching off through the trees at their right.

Helen slowed the car, glancing dubiously at the narrow lane revealed in the headlights' beam.

The boy sensed her indecision. "Don't worry," he said. "It's not far now."

Helen turned off into the opening between the trees, then turned the headlights up to bright as she steered a cautious course along the rutted roadway.

Beside her the boy glanced up again. "Are you moving to Willoughby?" he asked.

Helen glanced at him, amused. "You heard me say that, too, I guess."

He nodded. "How come you left Homewood?"

Helen hesitated, as for a moment her amusement faded. The little devil—he really *had* been listening! But that didn't give the kid the right to pry into her business.

Then again, what difference did it make? Might as well answer—if she could. Why had she left Homewood? A good question.

She shrugged, searching for the right words. "I don't know— I guess I was looking for something and didn't find it there."

The boy nodded. "What about your folks?"

"They're both gone."

"You mean they're dead?"

Helen nodded. "I'm afraid so."

"Oh." There was a note of concern in the small voice now. "Don't you have *anybody?*"

"Not anymore. I'm all alone."

Beside her the boy sat silent for a moment. Then, suddenly, he held out his hand, smiling.

"My name is Anthony," he said.

Helen released her right hand from the steering wheel and gripped the small palm in her own.

"Helen," she said.

Anthony turned gravely. "I'm very glad to meet you, Helen."

Now Helen turned her attention to the roadway once again. The car bumped along the narrow lane between the black border of towering trees.

"You really live quite aways out here, don't you?" Helen glanced down. "Your parents must be getting worried about you."

"Not really."

"No?"

Anthony shook his head. "They don't care when

I come home. I could come home at *midnight* and they wouldn't care."

Helen smiled at him indulgently. "Midnight, Anthony?"

"Yes." The boy paused for a moment, then continued. "It's my *birth*day today and they don't even care about *that!*"

Helen stared at him, startled. "You're kidding! Really?"

He nodded forlornly and her heart went out to him. "What a crummy birthday!"

"I'm okay." Anthony glanced up with a cheerful grin. "I made a friend."

Helen brightened. "Me too," she said.

Quite suddenly, the car emerged from the woods.

Peering through the windshield, Helen was surprised to see that the road ahead ran in a straight line between fields covered by parched grass. This was obviously farmland, but it lay fallow and unplanted, weeds its only crop. Under the dark and moonless sky, the horizon receded into deeper shadows without any evidence of lighted dwellings. It looked like the middle of nowhere.

Then, quite abruptly, the car's headlights focused on a white two-story house looming up directly ahead at the far end of the road.

As they approached, Helen noted that the architecture was Victorian, like something out of an old picture-book, rising from a complementary setting of green lawn surrounded by a white picket fence.

It seemed as out of place here as if it had been dropped from the sky.

Helen parked before the gateway, noting as she did so that there were lights faintly visible behind the closed shutters.

"Here we are," said Anthony.

They got out of the car and Helen moved around the side to join the boy as he started forward and opened the fence gate.

Together they moved up the walk bisecting the neat, well-trimmed lawn.

"What a lovely house!" Helen murmured.

Anthony seemed pleased by her reaction. "You like it?"

Helen nodded. "It's so peaceful. Way out here by itself."

Nearing the front door, Helen was surprised to see three cars standing in the shadows before the left-hand side of the structure. She couldn't make out details too clearly, but in the dim light she got a curious impression that they were coated with a fine layer of dust.

Anthony followed her gaze and she nodded toward him. "Three-car family, right?"

He smiled but made no reply. Stepping forward, he opened the front door. Chimes jangled faintly against a tinny background of music issuing from somewhere within.

Anthony gestured toward the open doorway. "C'mon in," he said.

Helen moved across the threshold and the boy followed her, closing the door behind him. They stood in a hallway lighted by old-fashioned wall lamps. A staircase rose directly ahead, leading to the floor above.

Now that the front door had closed, the music's fast jerky tempo was louder; it seemed to be coming from the doorway of the room down the hall at their left.

Anthony took Helen's hand and started toward it, then halted at the entrance just long enough for Helen to get a fleeting glimpse of the room beyond.

It was here that she discovered the source of the music: its ricky-ticky rhythm emanated from the television set against the far wall as cartoon figures leaped and bounded across the flickering screen.

Both the images on the tube and the television itself seemed oddly incongruous in this setting. The darkened parlor looked almost like a reproduction of a Currier and Ives print; the red plush carpet was heavy, the overstuffed furniture massive, the fireplace against the right wall surmounted by a huge marble mantel.

Now, rising from behind high-backed chairs placed directly before the television screen, an elderly man and a young girl turned toward the doorway with startled stares. For a moment Helen had the curious impression that both of them were less than pleased at this sudden invasion, but almost instantly their faces broke into bright, toothy smiles as they hurried forward, nodding at the boy beside her.

"Hi, Anthony!" They spoke simultaneously, then fell silent, turning their attention to Helen.

Again she sensed a momentary reaction of uneasiness in their glances, but it was quickly dispelled as their smiles returned.

Beside her, the small, dark-haired boy nodded, his brown eyes fixed upon their faces. "This is Helen," he said.

The elderly man's features creased into a genial grin. "Helen! Delighted to meet you! Any friend of Anthony's—"

"Hello there!" The girl's voice rose over his as she nodded at their visitor.

"This is Uncle Walt and my sister, Ethel," Anthony said.

Helen smiled. "How do you do?"

In the moment that followed, she had an opportunity to sort out her impressions, noting that Uncle Walt must be in his early sixties. Although he wore a checkered sport shirt and casual blue jeans, his trendy attire could not conceal the stooped shoulders and the thinness of his limbs. In contrast, Ethel was quite plump; she appeared to be about sixteen, and the bulging body beneath her blouse and skirt betokened the results of overindulgence in junk food. Her face, framed by long strands of lusterless blond hair, wore a bovine look.

Helen's quick appraisal was interrupted by the sound of voices from the hallway behind.

"Did I hear Anthony come in"

The high-pitched query was met by a booming, deeper-toned response. "Yes, indeedy! There he is!"

Helen turned, stepping aside as another couple

entered the room. Both were in their forties; the woman wearing a blouse and slacks, her companion's garments similar to those of Uncle Walt.

Anthony nodded up at them. "This is my mother and father."

Helen concealed her surprise with a hasty smile; somehow they seemed a trifle too old to have a son of Anthony's age. "Pleased to meet you," she said.

Anthony gestured toward her. "This is Helen."

His mother beamed. "Helen! Delighted!"

The man grinned, reaching out to take her hand and pump it in warm welcome. "Pleased to meet you, young lady!"

"She gave me a ride home," Anthony announced.

The response was overwhelming, rising from all sides.

"*Did* she now?"

"How nice!"

"Wonderful!"

"Very sweet of her to go to all that trouble!"

Helen glanced up awkwardly at the circle of jolly faces surrounding her.

"I'm afraid we had a little accident," she murmured.

"Accident?" Anthony's mother was still smiling, but her voice held a hint of uncertainty.

Now they were all staring at Helen, and she sensed a curious concern behind their genial smiles. Rendered self-conscious by their scrutiny, she hurried on, her voice faltering. "I—I knocked Anthony down while he was riding his bicycle."

"Oh?" Anthony's mother continued to smile, but her voice again betrayed her.

Ethel's agitation was even more evident. "Knocked him *down?*"

Her father glanced at her, then spoke quickly. "Well! It doesn't look like any harm was done!"

"No, *sir!*" Uncle Walt nodded heartily. "Anthony looks fine!"

"I hope so," Helen murmured.

Father nodded at the boy, his eyes twinkling. "Oh yes! Anthony looks fine to me!"

The boy turned toward his mother. "Can Helen stay for supper?"

"Oh, no!" Helen shook her head quickly. "I wouldn't dream of imposing—"

"Imposing?" Anthony's mother was speaking again. "Not at all—I think it's a wonderful idea!"

"Marvelous!" Her husband chuckled his approval. "Of course she can!"

Helen smiled politely. For a moment she was still tempted to refuse, but the anxious expectancy in Anthony's eyes won her over; she didn't have the heart to turn him down.

"Thank you," she said.

"Good!" His father looked relieved. "Then, it's all settled."

Anthony looked up at his mother. "Can we eat right now?"

"Why, yes—of course."

Helen turned to her. "If you don't mind, I'd like to wash up first."

Anthony said, "Sure," and nodded eagerly toward the doorway. "I'll show you where."

"Thank you." Helen turned and followed him from the room.

His mother's voice sped them on their way. "See you in a little while!"

Anthony led Helen down the hall, then started up the stairs. "This way, Helen."

From below, the squawk and squeak of meaningless musical merriment echoed forth. With a start Helen realized that the televised cartoons were continuing; they'd been running constantly while she'd been in the parlor. But now, as she and Anthony reached the upper landing, the sounds gave way to silence.

The boy started along the hall to the right. Helen moved up beside him. "I like your folks, Anthony," she said.

"Do you?" His voice was flat, noncommittal.

"Of course." Helen smiled down into his sober face. "And how could you possibly say they don't care about you? Come on!"

Anthony glanced up, frowning. "They *don't!*"

Helen shrugged. "Well, *my* family was never this happy to see me in my whole life!"

"They aren't like that, Helen. Not really."

Reaching the end of the hallway, he turned right and into another corridor. Somewhat to her surprise, Helen noted the absence of any doorway here; come to think of it, she hadn't seen any in the other passageway.

She frowned, puzzled. "Anthony—where are we going?"

A low rumbling, something like an animal growl, sounded from behind the wall at their left and Helen halted quickly.

So did the sound.

She glanced around, confused. "What in the world was that?"

"What?" Anthony seemed undisturbed.

"Didn't you hear the noise?"

Anthony cocked his head, listening for a moment. "I don't hear anything." He reached out and took her hand. "Come on."

As they started forward, Helen noticed an opening at her right; there *were* rooms up here after all. Passing the open doorway, Helen glanced inside.

The bedroom beyond was dark, save for the illumination from the tube of a TV console in one corner. Sitting in a wheelchair, facing away from the door, Helen caught a fleeting glimpse of a teenage girl. Motionless, oblivious of their presence, she stared intently at the cartoon on the screen. Now, as barks and growls arose, Helen realized the origin of the sound that had startled her.

Then Anthony's hand tugged her forward past the doorway. "That's Sarah," he said. "She's my other sister."

"I noticed she's in a wheelchair," Helen said.

"Yeah." Anthony nodded shortly. "She was in an accident." Then he gestured to indicate a door at the end of the hall ahead. "Here's the bathroom."

*   *   *

Almost five minutes elapsed before Helen finished what she judged to be the absolute minimum of necessary repairs to her makeup and coiffure. Anthony was awaiting her outside the bathroom door. As they passed along the hall, she noticed that the door to his sister's room was closed now; he must have visited the girl during the time she was fixing her face.

Helen was about to inquire concerning the nature of Sarah's accident but Anthony, gripping her hand firmly, seemed anxious to get downstairs again as quickly as possible.

To her surprise the family was still gathered in the parlor, grouped around the television set as it spewed forth yet another in a series of seemingly endless cartoons.

A giant cat wearing an old-fashioned burglar's mask tiptoed stealthily across a rooftop and crawled into a chimney to invade the dwelling below. Inside the house two mice, wearing the clothing of human youngsters, were busily kindling a gigantic blaze in the fireplace. The cat came sailing down the chimney shaft, landing butt-first in the fire. A burst of mocking music indicated just how hilarious it was to see an animal in danger of incineration; a loud *yeow!* heightened the mirthful aspect of the scene as the cat shot up the chimney shaft on the rebound. To cap the jest, he emerged from the chimney with such speed that there was no way of checking his momentum. Soaring high above the rooftop to the screeching accompaniment of off-key violins, he bounced against an overhead power line to the sound of the inevitable *boing!* Jagged streaks of electricity shooting out from his furry form, he burst into flame, then plummeted to earth, landing on a concrete driveway with an obligatory thump, followed by the cracking of the stone and, presumably, his skull.

Helen diverted her attention from the screen to survey its audience. Despite the high comedy afforded by the cat burglar's sufferings, Anthony's family didn't seem amused. In the dim light from the picture tube, their faces loomed drawn and haggard.

But it was only a trick of the light. As Anthony entered the room, they turned toward him instantly, wearing smiles of welcome.

"We're ready to eat now," he announced.

Over the sound of the cartoon, a chorus of enthusiastic agreement arose.

"Good!"

"Wonderful!"

"Great!"

"You bet!"

Listening to the varying voices, Helen was reminded of a childhood fairy tale. "The Three Bears," that was it; Papa and Mama and Baby Bear, inquiring "Who's been sleeping in my bed?"

Stupid, of course; there were four here and they weren't bears, nor had she been sleeping in any of their beds.

Maybe it was the cartoons that made her think of fairy tales. In any case, her attention was diverted now as the family gathered around Anthony like a squad of soldiers awaiting the command of their leader.

They do love him! she told herself. Helen had never seen such devotion, such anxiety to please a youngster; even his sister deferred. Obviously there was no sibling rivalry here. But catering to him could lead to unpleasant consequences; Anthony might easily end up a spoiled brat.

Helen hoped she was wrong. Glancing down at the child, she felt the stirrings of emotional response, an unaccountable desire to protect him. But from what? He seemed totally at ease, and as he turned to her, the sober little face broke into a warm smile in which all her apprehension melted.

"Let's eat here," he said. "Then we won't have to miss the cartoons."

Uncle Walt nodded. "Hey! That's a great idea! Why didn't we think of that ourselves?"

"Sounds good to me." Father nodded. "I'll go get us the card table. We can set it up right over here."

"Better hurry," Uncle Walt chuckled. "I bet Anthony's mighty hungry!"

He left the room and it seemed scarcely moments before he returned, lugging the table.

Anthony's mother beamed at Helen. "We're very happy you can eat with us. Anthony's so thoughtful that way."

As she spoke, Helen realized that the sound-track of the cartoon had faded. Now Anthony's voice was clearly audible.

"Would you like to sit next to me, Helen?"

She turned, noting with surprise that the boy was seated on a small sofa directly facing the TV screen. Funny she hadn't noticed the sofa before. Now, meeting Anthony's expectant gaze, she hesitated. "Well, maybe your mother will want to sit there . . ."

"No—no, you go ahead." Anthony's mother nodded. "I have to get supper."

His father had finished unfolding the legs of the card table and now he set it up at one side, arranging the chairs around it. "This will be fine," he said. "The rest of us can eat here—you just sit right next to Anthony."

Helen settled down beside the boy. He smiled at her quickly, then turned his attention to the screen before him.

Poised on the edge of a precipice, a rabbit pushed a huge boulder over the edge and watched with a grin as it landed directly on the head of an unsuspecting bear below. A loud crash indicated that the volume on the sound-track had risen again. Helen frowned, puzzled; maybe something was wrong with the controls. Then she glanced up as Anthony's mother appeared beside him, bending forward as she spoke.

"Darling—"

He glanced up, annoyed by this distraction, to meet her nervous smile.

"I don't mean to interrupt you, dear, but—"

"But what?"

The nervous smile wavered before his irritated gaze. "It's just, well—do you happen to remember where supper is?"

Helen stared at her blankly. What kind of a question was *that?* But Anthony was frowning.

"You know where it is."

His mother's smile had disappeared completely now. "I *do?*"

Anthony nodded. "It's in the *oven*, isn't it, Mother?"

"Oh! Of course!" Mother's smile returned, accompanied by a laugh that conveyed both relief and embarrassment. "How silly of me!"

Behind her, Anthony's father chuckled.

So did Uncle Walt.

"She never knows." He gave Helen a wink, shaking his head.

Mother moved toward the doorway and Anthony's father fell into step beside her. "I'll help you get things ready," he told her.

Sister Ethel started after them. "Me too! I can't wait to see what we have tonight!"

Helen watched them exit, then turned to Anthony, her glance questioning. He shrugged, then smiled hesitantly.

"It's a game," he said.

Conscious of the skepticism in her stare, he swallowed hard, then continued. "It's all pretend! She knows where supper is. She just wants to see if I can guess."

Uncle Walt moved beside him, nodding cheerily. "That's right, just a little game!"

Helen framed another question, but before she could speak, her attention was distracted by a sudden burst of sound from the television.

On-screen a worried wolf seated in the open cockpit of a small plane watched in panic as the wings fell off and the propeller dropped away. The plane spun into a nose dive, spiraling through the clouds and crashed in flames. Now the wolf reeled forth from an inferno of smoke, his frazzled fur singed and smoking.

Beside her, Anthony's laugh rose in approval. "This is a good cartoon."

"Uh-huh." Helen forced a smile. "But aren't there some other programs you like to watch, too?"

Anthony shook his head. "Cartoons are the best." He pointed at the screen, where the wolf's smoking figure suddenly melted into the form of a ghostly angel, a halo encircling its head and a harp appearing between its paws. Now, spreading celestial wings, it floated away.

"You see?" Anthony nodded happily. "Anything can happen in cartoons."

He turned to face Helen again. "That's why I like them. Don't you?" The brown eyes were serious now, as he gazed up expectantly. Helen sensed that somehow he attached great importance to her answer.

She shifted in her seat, oddly disconcerted by his stare. "Well . . . I guess everybody likes cartoons."

"Not everybody." Anthony darted a disapproving glance at his uncle.

Uncle Walt chuckled hastily. "Oh, sure we do! We *all* like cartoons! Anything can happen in 'em, just like Anthony says. Wouldn't want to watch anything else, no-siree!"

Now footsteps sounded from the hallway, and a voice rose gaily. "Here we come!"

Helen turned, gazing over the back of the sofa as Anthony's parents appeared followed by Ethel, each of them carrying two cardboard plates.

"Good stuff here for everybody!" Father grinned happily as he set his burden down on the card table. Ethel followed suit, then lugged a small end table across the room and set it down before the sofa where Anthony's mother stood waiting.

"There you are, darling." Mother put down one plate before him, then placed the other before his guest.

"Thank you," Helen murmured.

As his mother moved away to join the others seated around the card table, Anthony turned his attention to the food.

Helen glanced down at her plate, staring dubiously at its contents.

What kind of a meal was this? A thin hamburger and a jelly donut nestled against a candy bar and a bag of potato chips. Was this their idea of good food? Apparently so, for from the card table across the room, voices rose in ecstatic approval.

"Mmm! Doesn't this look *yummy?*"

"Boy, that's good!"

"Isn't this delicious!"

"You *bet!*"

Anthony cast a sidelong glance at Helen. "Okay?"

Helen nodded politely. She was conscious of guarded stares from the other table as she lifted the hamburger bun. To her surprise there was peanut butter smeared on top of the meat patty.

The boy beamed at her. "I always like peanut butter on hamburgers. It's good that way."

She managed a smile as she put the top back on the bun and took a tentative nibble. The silent tension at the other table was broken now by the sounds of enjoyment; the lip-smacking noises and enthusiastic murmurs with which food is consumed in television commercials.

As she listened, vagrant thoughts intruded. There had been no commercials interrupting the TV cartoons here tonight. That was strange. But even stranger was the spectacle of Anthony's family devouring their odd meal as though it were a gourmet dinner.

Helen forced herself to take another tiny bite. Yes, it was all very strange; now another thought occurred. She glanced at Anthony and framed a question.

"Isn't your sister Sarah going to eat with us?"

Anthony seemed taken aback. "Uh, no. Sarah doesn't eat."

Mirthful assent rose from the foursome around the card table.

"That's right!"

"Sarah doesn't eat, no way!"

"That's *funny,* Anthony!"

"Every time he says that, I get such a kick!"

Anthony frowned. Instantly they fell silent. A moment later the murmurs of party enjoyment resumed, but Helen was conscious of their wariness; it, too, raised a question, and she was tired of questions. What she needed were a few straight answers.

She turned to the boy. "Do you always eat like this?"

Anthony did not reply and Helen was acutely conscious of the sudden silence from the other table. They were all staring at her now.

Mother was the first to speak, her thin smile belied by the apprehension in her voice. "Anthony can have anything he wants."

Father nodded quickly. "Anything at all!"

Uncle Walt forced an unconvincing chuckle. "You *bet* he can!"

Helen ignored them; she was waiting for the boy to speak.

He nodded at her apologetically. "Don't you think it's good?"

Helen hesitated. Politeness dictated an approving response, but she was sick of politeness, sick of phony approval, sick of this strange overprotective atmosphere and the unanswered questions it posed. Couldn't the family understand what they were doing to the child by indulging him this way? Didn't they realize the consequences of catering to his whims? Maybe it was none of her business, perhaps she was reverting to her role as a schoolteacher, but it was time somebody spoke up.

She nodded quickly. "I suppose it's all right once in a while," she told him, "but you're young, you need to get proper nutrition." She fixed the family with a stare of pedagogical disapproval. "You can't eat like this *all* the time!"

Flustered, Anthony shook his head. "I never thought of that. But you're right, Helen. It's *not* good all the time—"

Again the echoing chorus rose from the other table.

"Right! Anthony's a growing boy!"

"Of course he is! He needs his nutrition."

"You're *so* right, Anthony!"

Anthony turned, silencing them with an accusing stare. "You'd *never* tell me that," he cried.

Their smiles were sickly, but no one spoke. It remained for Helen to break the mood.

"Oh well," she murmured. "I really shouldn't be criticizing, should I?" She smiled at the youngster. "After all, it *is* your birthday supper."

Again, the terrible silence. And then Ethel's voice, rising almost despairingly. *"Another* birthday?"

Uncle Walt's grin was gone. "With *presents?*"

Anthony shook his head angrily. "No—it's not my birthday! I never told you that—"

As he gestured toward them, the group around the table recoiled, catching their breaths.

Shrinking back, Ethel's elbow knocked against the side of her plate, spilling it to the floor.

Anthony glowered at her. "Stop that!" he cried. "I'm not doing anything." Then he caught himself, turning to Helen and forcing his smile. "They're being silly!"

Helen faced him, speaking softly. "Anthony, you did tell me it was your birthday."

Mother's voice rose in a dreadful parody of cheer. "Of course it is!"

"Yes!" Ethel chimed in immediately.

So did Uncle Walt. "Sure! We all know it's Anthony's birthday, don't we?"

His valiant attempt at a chuckle emerged, but it sounded more like a frightened cackle of sheer panic, halting abruptly as Anthony shouted him down.

"It's *not!* I told you it's not my birthday, do you hear?"

Helen stared in shock at the family's frightened faces. What was wrong with them, what had she started here? She didn't know the answer, but whatever it might be, it didn't matter to her now. Suddenly all she wanted was out of here.

She started to rise from the sofa. "I think I'd better go, Anthony."

Anthony gazed up at her hastily, eyes imploring. "No!"

The passion in his voice made Helen stiffen.

Now the boy rose, his eyes beseeching. "Please —it's okay, everything's okay."

He glanced at the television screen, where a cartoon rabbit was climbing out of a magician's hat. "You gotta stay," he said. "Uncle Walt's gonna do a trick for us."

"I'm sorry, Anthony." Helen shook her head. "I really must leave now."

"But Uncle Walt's gonna do a trick—just for *you!* Please—sit down—"

"You bet!" Uncle Walt nodded but Helen ignored him and started to turn away.

Anthony put his hand on her arm. "It only takes a minute. You'll see—" As she halted, the boy called out quickly, "Do the hat trick, Uncle Walt! The hat trick!"

"You bet!" Uncle Walt rose, then stared blankly around the room. His booming voice faltered. "Where—where's the hat?"

"Over *there*." Anthony released his grip on Helen's arm, gesturing impulsively. "On the TV set."

Automatically Helen's gaze followed his pointing finger. Resting on the TV set was a top hat.

Helen stared in surprise, but as she did so she was conscious of another and more unsettling emotion rising within her; something akin to panic.

Anthony smiled up at her reassuringly. "You'll like this."

Helen took a deep breath. "Anthony—"

The boy ignored her. "Go ahead, Uncle Walt," he called.

"Yes, sir!"

As Helen watched, Uncle Walt moved slowly across the room and reached out to pick up the top hat. He grasped it hesitantly, the gesture of a man forcing himself to pick up a live coal from the fire.

But Anthony was nodding happily. "You'll like this, Helen. It's good." Before she could move again, he grabbed her hand squeezing it tightly, then turned to call. *"Do* it, Uncle Walt. Do it now!"

The intensity in his voice was matched by that of

his grip. Helen stood motionless, watching as he clutched her hand.

Now everyone was watching as Uncle Walt turned, hat in hand. His attempt at a smile was horrible to see, but Anthony's eyes were fixed upon him in inexorable command.

Slowly, Uncle Walt reached down into the hat. A moment later his hand emerged again, holding up a white rabbit.

Helen could sense his suppressed shudder of relief as he faced the family with a ghastly grin. "Ta-da!" he muttered shakily.

Their response of mingled handclaps and laughter was no more convincing than Uncle Walt's grin, but Anthony gazed up at Helen now. "Isn't this fun? We do it a lot. You'd like it here, Helen, honest you would."

Helen stared at him, her panic mounting and from behind her rose an insane babble of agreement from the rest of the family.

"You'd *love* it here! You would!"

Helen stared at them in sudden dread, then jerked her hand free. She had to get out, had to—

Anthony, sensing her intention, shouted to Uncle Walt. "Do it again! Do it *right!*"

Before Helen could turn away, Uncle Walt's hand descended into the hat, then drew back, gasping. Eyes frantic with fear, he watched as an enormous figure rose to tower above the television set.

It was a rabbit—but not the sort that a professional stage magician could conjure up. Only a sorcerer could summon such a thing. This was a multicolored monstrosity, a huge misshapen creature with the paws and claws of a tiger. Great yellow eyes bulged above a snouted muzzle, which gaped wide now, revealing a long snakelike tongue lolling forth from between the curved fangs of a sabretooth. Squatting atop the television set, the thing extended its talons.

Helen cried out, raising her hand as a shield against the sight.

As she did so, Anthony gestured swiftly. "Don't be scared!" he shouted.

He gestured again, this time in the direction of the television set. Helen lowered her arm just in time to see the entity spiral down and vanish into the hat once more. An instant later, the hat itself had disappeared.

Blindly, unmindful of the family's reaction, intent only on frantic flight, Helen turned and grabbed her purse from the end table near the doorway. To her dismay its clasp opened and the bag slipped from her trembling fingers, its contents spilling across the floor.

She knelt quickly, trying to capture the items scattering across the carpet.

Anthony crouched beside her, shaking his head in anguish. "I didn't *want* to do that! Honest I didn't— I just got mad, and sometimes I can't help what happens!"

Helen made no reply, but the look on her face was answer enough. Now the boy began to assist her, picking up objects and stuffing them back into her purse. And all the while his soft, intense voice sounded through the silence.

"Please don't go, Helen! I can make it real nice here. I can make the food the way you said it should be. I can even change the *house* if you want! Just say it, and I can make anything you like, but don't—"

Suddenly he broke off, looking closely at a scrap of paper he had picked up from the floor. Now the pleading face was transformed into a mask of rage.

Helen stared at him, startled. As Anthony scrambled to his feet, the family cowered back against the wall. Still glaring, the boy turned to Helen and held out the scrap of paper.

"You see?" he said. "I told you how they were!"

Helen glanced down at the crumpled fragment, which appeared to be torn from the upper margin of a newspaper. Across its length read the words of the hastily scrawled pencil message:

Help us! Anthony is a Monster!

She glanced up as he nodded. "They *hate* me! They want to send me away to someplace bad, just like my *real* mother and father did!"

Voices faltered forth from the far end of the room. "That's not true, Anthony—"

"Of course not—"

"You know how we—"

The three responses sounded simultaneously and Anthony cut them off with a single wave. He turned to Helen, speaking rapidly. "They're afraid of me. Everybody is. That's why they act this way. And I do *everything* for them! They can watch TV all day.

152

No one has to do a thing. Not a thing! I'm real good all the time—"

Uncle Walt's voice sounded in hasty agreement. "That's right—Anthony's a *good* boy. We love him!"

The youngster reached out, plucking the piece of paper from between Helen's trembling fingers. Rising, he moved toward the four figures cowering against the far wall, their eyes terrified by the threat in his.

"Then I wonder who wrote this note." Now the threat entered his voice. "I wonder who called me a monster?"

Instantly the babble began. *"He* did it!"

"Not me!"

"You know *I* didn't do it! It was Ethel!"

"Yes—Ethel. *She's* the one!"

Mother, Father, and Uncle Walt were all pointing now, pointing at the stricken girl. She shook her head, eyes widening, mouth twitching in terror.

Helen rose. She didn't know what Anthony intended; only that somehow, whatever it was, he had to be stopped.

Anthony was nodding at the girl. "Oh? I didn't know that. What a big surprise! Ethel, huh?"

Ethel shook her head frantically. Her voice was shaking, too. "All right! Go ahead and do it—*do it*—"

The boy smiled at her now and his whisper was almost gentle. "Do what, Ethel?"

Somehow this mockery held even more menace than his rage. With a convulsive effort, Ethel tore

153

her gaze free from his accusing stare and gestured at Helen, her words tumbling out in a haste born of hysteria.

"Now do you realize you'll never get away?" she shouted. "You think it was an accident you came here? He *made* it happen! He brought you here just like he brought us here and kept us! Just the way he'll keep you!" She nodded, but her voice raced on.

"Or maybe he'll get mad at you someday like he did with his *real* sister and cripple you and take away your mouth so you can't yell at him, or maybe do what he did to his *real* mother and father—"

For an instant Anthony closed his eyes, wincing in pain. Then he opened them once more, staring at the girl. Softly, very softly, he spoke:

"Time for you to go now, Ethel."

Helen took a step forward. "Anthony, don't—"

But Anthony ignored her. He faced Ethel, smiling his secret smile.

"It's a special surprise. I just made it up."

Ethel moaned, shaking her head as Anthony's voice rose. "I'm wishing you to *Cartoonland!*"

Ethel vanished.

Not in a puff of smoke. Not in a blind flash. She simply—disappeared.

Helen stood frozen. Ice water trickled in her veins, her limbs were numb with cold, but it was not physical chill that set her trembling. This wasn't the first time she had seen someone disappear before her very eyes; she'd watched magic acts on the stage, where the conjurer waved his wand and a shapely assistant had seemingly vanished from behind a black cloth or the confines of a closed cabinet. And in fantasy films a wizard might mutter an incantation that caused another character to fade from the screen. But this prosaically furnished parlor was not a stage set and the small boy standing before her wasn't a magician. He hadn't waved a wand or uttered a spell and Ethel had not been obliterated by means of a movie's special effects.

This was reality. The parlor was real. The people in it, including Ethel, actually existed.

Or *had* existed. Because now Ethel was gone. A small boy uttered a simple sentence and Ethel became a nonperson.

It was the cold reality that sent shivers along Helen's spine.

And now the small boy was smiling at her.

"I told you cartoons are good," Anthony said. "Anything can happen in them!"

He turned, pointing toward the television set.

Helen followed his gaze to the screen, where animated figures of goblins and witches were chasing their victim. Now the object of their pursuit glanced back and Helen stared in shock at the familiar face.

Ethel was in the cartoon!

For a moment her panic-stricken features filled the screen, mouth opened to sound a shriek, which rose against a blaring background of merry music.

Then Anthony's hand rose in a sweeping gesture,

for all the world like one of Helen's former pupils using an eraser to wipe a blackboard clean.

The screen went blank.

And Anthony, in a dreadful parody of Bugs Bunny, stuttered *"Th-th-th-th-that's all, Ethel!"*

With a gasp, Helen turned and ran for the door. Behind her she heard the family's cries, heard the boy's sharply shouted command, but she didn't look back.

Now, racing down the hall, she reached the front door and tugged at the handle. For one fearful moment she thought it was locked; then, suddenly surrendering to her strength, it flew open.

Helen started forward, only to stumble back as a huge gust of wind roared through the doorway from the darkness beyond. Reeling, she forced herself forward again but as she did so, something rolled through the darkness to bar her path.

Filling the threshold before her was a gigantic staring eyeball.

Helen slammed the door and twisted around, sobbing.

Half-blinded by tears of mingled frustration and frantic fear, she watched Anthony advancing toward her down the hallway. The anger had drained from his face; now his expression was one of contrition and concern.

"I can't help it, Helen," he said. "I don't *want* to hurt anybody. If you'll just come back—"

He reached out and took her hand. Almost without realizing it, Helen found herself moving with him along the hall.

Through her sobs she heard his voice sounding plaintively.

"You don't understand. Nobody does. All I have to do is wish for something and it happens."

Now they were in the parlor once more. Blinking away her tears, Helen looked up and saw the family still huddled motionless against the far wall, paralyzed with shock. Beside her, Anthony was still speaking.

"Please, Helen, you've got to believe me! I can do anything. *Anything!*"

As if to demonstrate, he turned toward the silent television set. The group against the wall stared speechless in agonized expectation. Despite herself, Helen was staring, too.

And now the television set started to vibrate. Sparks flew forth from the screen. The cabinet began to glow, incandescent with an inner energy that enveloped it in flickering flame. With a hideous grating screech, the top of the set ripped apart, bursting before a force that boiled upward from within.

Then the opening widened splitting the set in half. A whirling, snarling form spun upward, streaming out into the room and enlarging as it emerged. The swirling figure was that of a cartoon dragon, but as it grew, it changed into something far more horrifying —something three-dimensional—a living, pulsating reality. Its eyes were gigantic glaring globes of fire and its breath was a jet of flame.

Helen swayed back, closing her eyes. "Wish it away, Anthony!" she panted. *"Wish it away!"*

A surging sound rose. Helen forced her eyes open as with blinding speed the huge form dwindled, collapsing back into the yawning fissure of the shattered television set. Then, with a final flicker, it shimmered away, together with the ruined remnants of the set itself.

There was a moment of utter silence.

Helen stared at the family cringing against the wall, stared at the boy beside her. He too was surveying the room, and when at last he turned toward her, his face was a mask of misery.

"I hate this house," he murmured. "I hate everything about it."

Suffused with sudden purpose, his voice rose.

"I wish it *all* away!"

Succumbing to dreadful impulse, Helen turned her gaze toward the figures cowering against the wall. Again, no spells were uttered, no wands waved. But as she watched, one by one, they all disappeared.

Mother, Father, Uncle Walt, vanished into—

Nothingness.

The room itself had melted away. Helen turned, her eyes searching the darkness, finding nothing but the night surrounding her on all sides. Nothing but the night—and Anthony, standing beside her in empty space.

"Where—where are we?" she faltered.

Anthony stared at her bleakly. "Nowhere."

Helen's voice echoed through emptiness. "Where are the others?"

"I sent them wherever they wanted to go." Anthony's voice trembled. "Away from me."

Helen looked down at the boy. Suddenly, standing here in the darkness, he seemed utterly helpless, utterly forlorn. There was nothing monstrous about him now—all she saw was a lost, lonely little boy. Bracing herself, she took him by the shoulder and bent forward, meeting his gaze eye-to-eye.

"Anthony," she whispered. "Take us back."

The child's stare wavered. "So *you* can leave, too?"

She sensed the accusation in his voice, but his eyes held only hopelessness and his face was white with fear.

Helen hesitated, then took a deep breath.

"I won't leave you," she said. "Take us back, Anthony. Take us back, so you and I can try again."

The boy stared at her without speaking, his eyes shining with sudden hope, then dulling in doubt and despair.

Helen shook her head. "I'm not lying to you, Anthony." Now the words came unbidden, from somewhere deep within her. "You need someone to teach you. Somebody to help you understand this gift you have—this terrible, *wonderful* gift. A gift you must control. We must learn how to use it wisely." She took another deep breath. "The two of us can learn together."

Anthony looked up anxiously. "You'll stay with me?"

"Yes."

"Always?"

Helen nodded; there was no turning back. "Always."

Anthony smiled. "Okay," he said.

Reaching out, he took her hand. For a moment they stood together in the darkness. Then something flickered, and the emptiness around them was filled with recognizable reality once more.

Utter blackness faded into the ordinary shadows of normal light. Looking around, Helen saw that she and Anthony were standing on the same spot formerly occupied by the house. It was gone now, but surrounding her were the barren fields through which she had driven, and in the distance she recognized the road that wound its way back into the bordering trees.

Smiling in relief, she waited for Anthony to speak.

He nodded quickly. "Let's go."

Helen turned, then halted, frowning.

Although the house was gone, the driveway before it was still intact. Intact and empty—her car was nowhere to be seen.

For a moment Helen hesitated, remembering her own words. This was a new beginning; they must learn together, learn how to control Anthony's power, using it only to serve its proper purpose. She must be careful not to encourage any further demonstrations until they both were sure what the consequences might be. On the other hand, they *did* need wheels in order to leave here in an ordinary fashion.

Helen made her decision, lips framing a question. "My car—?"

Anthony smiled, then made a small offhand gesture.

Instantly the car was back in the driveway, parked directly before them.

"Okay?" Anthony smiled at her. "Can we go now?"

Helen nodded. Together they moved to the car and Helen opened the door, waiting while Anthony slid across to the right-hand passenger-seat. Then she took her place before the wheel, closing the door behind her.

Suddenly she frowned and the boy glanced up at her questioningly.

"What's the matter?"

Helen shook her head. "I forgot." She gestured toward the ignition. "I don't have the key—it's in my purse—"

But as she spoke, something flicked between her fingers. Staring down, she saw the car key nestling in her palm; at the same moment she sensed the pressure of her purse against her lap.

Anthony was smiling.

Helen sighed, shaking her head in mingled relief and admonition. "Let's not do too much of that anymore," she murmured.

"Okay," said Anthony.

Helen started the engine, then headed the car back down the road leading to the trees. As she did so, she found herself making mental notes. She really must do something about Anthony's vocabulary—he'd just said "okay" three times in five minutes; and she would have to teach him something about grooming—his hair was badly in need of combing, and that soiled outfit he wore was a positive disgrace.

Somehow the prospect didn't dismay her—if anything, the thought of teaching again filled her with joyful anticipation.

So much to teach, so much to learn—

Helen glanced at Anthony and he smiled, his face radiant with a happiness so great that he seemed unable to contain it. Beaming up at her, he made a little gesture with both his hands.

Suddenly the sky brightened into morning sunlight and as Helen stared wide-eyed through the windshield, the bare fields bordering the road ahead blossomed out into bright and shining banks of flowers.

Helen shook her head reprovingly. "Anthony!"

But as she spoke, she smiled.

Anthony smiled with her. The whole world was smiling now as the car sped through the fields of flowers and into the twilight of the trees beyond.

4

BLOOM

The afternoon sun was just beginning to fade as Mr. Bloom walked through the doorway.

Miss Cox looked up from her seat behind the reception desk, then nodded briskly.

"Here we are!" She rose and moved forward with a smile of greeting that was as false as her teeth. "I've been expecting you all afternoon, Mr. Bloom."

"Sorry to be so late, " Bloom said. "But how did you know who I am?"

Even as he spoke, he knew the answer. After all, he had given his name over the telephone when applying for admission and told her to expect him on Saturday afternoon. So when a man his age walked in carrying a suitcase, all she had to do was put two and two together. Or one and one. He wasn't very good at numbers, and besides, it didn't matter.

Neither did her reply, but he listened politely just the same.

"I formed a mental picture when we talked on the phone the other day," she said. "I find my intuitions seldom fail me in that regard." She stared at him quizzically, pale gray eyes narrowing behind the lenses of rimless spectacles. "You're a Pisces, aren't you?"

Bloom was definitely not a Pisces, but he shook his head in wonder. "Remarkable," he murmured. "Absolutely remarkable!"

Miss Cox's sallow cheeks flushed with pride. "Nothing to it," she declared. "Just a matter of practice and observation. Working in a retirement home like this, you see so many people come and go—"

She broke off hastily now, abruptly aware of the unfortunate connotation of her remark, but Bloom pretended he hadn't noticed.

"Enough of that," Miss Cox was saying. "Welcome to Sunneyvale!"

Raising her left wrist, she glanced down quickly

at the watch that rested atop it. "My goodness, it *is* getting late! We'd better get you squared away before it's time for your din-din."

Turning, she started down the hall and Mr. Bloom fell into step beside her. An observer might have found them a curious combination: the tall bony woman in the nurse's uniform towering over the frail little old man at her side. The frail little old man was still carrying his suitcase; Miss Cox had not offered to relieve him of his burden.

As they moved down the hallway, Mr. Bloom glanced curiously through the open doorway on his left.

The room was large, large enough to contain half a dozen beds. Above each was a small shelf and against the opposite wall stood six identical plywood storage cabinets, apparently used to house wardrobes and personal belongings. Beside every bed was a single chair, only two of which were occupied.

"That's our ladies' dormitory," Miss Cox told him. "As you can see, we don't have a full house at the moment. There were four here until last week, when Mrs. Schanfarber passed away. And Mrs. Tomkins is in the infirmary now. Poor thing. Dr. Ryan looked in on her last night. Says she has viral pneumonia. Just between us, I'm afraid she isn't going to make it."

Bloom glanced at the two seated ladies, both of whom were eating dinner from trays set atop the small folding chairs before them.

One wore an elaborate housecoat trimmed with

an overabundance of ribbons and lace. It was the sort of garment that might be chosen by a girl in her twenties who had just told a visiting boyfriend that she wanted to slip into something more comfortable. But this lady was at least fifty years removed from girlhood; although her white hair was curled tightly by the recent application of a home-permanent and her sunken cheeks had been heavily rouged, Bloom judged her to be well into her seventies.

"That's Mrs. Dempsey," the nurse told him. "She's a widow." Now her smile soured into disapproval as she gestured toward the long-haired white cat snuggling in Mrs. Dempsey's lap. "And that's Mickey, " she said. "I keep telling her not to feed him from the table, but she doesn't pay any attention."

Bloom nodded, staring at the other occupant of the dormitory. She was a plump, neatly dressed woman with dark hair and a jolly expression; the hair was obviously a wig, but her smile was genuine.

Miss Cox followed his gaze. "That's Mrs. Weinstein. Would you believe it, she's over eighty and still going strong. Her husband is with us, too. Of course, he's in the men's dormitory. They spend a lot of time together, but we don't have a regular dining room here, so we prefer our residents to take their meals separately. You know how it is. If they all ate together, there'd be too much confusion. Besides, some of them are on special diets." A slight frown creased her forehead. "For example, the Weinsteins only eat Kosher. You can't imagine the trouble that makes in the kitchen."

Bloom nodded again, but listening to Miss Cox's remarks about the residents made him just a trifle uncomfortable; he felt like a visitor being taken on a guided tour of the zoo by the head keeper.

Now they moved along the hall to another open doorway at the right. He followed Miss Cox over the threshold and found himself in a room almost identical to the one that the women occupied.

"This is the men's dormitory," Miss Cox announced. "I've given you the first bed here, nearest the door. Weinstein likes the one next to the window—he's had it for years. Seniority rights, you know." She glanced along the row of empty beds. "Agee is next to Weinstein and then comes Conroy. And Mute in the one next to you."

Bloom stared down the row of empty beds. "Don't the men eat here?"

"Usually they do," Miss Cox said. "But seeing as this is Saturday, Weinstein and Agee are having dinner with Mute in the recreation room. They like to watch the game on television there. And Conroy is in the visitors' room with his son and daughter-in-law."

Bloom noticed that she referred to none of the men as "Mr." Obviously Miss Cox was an ardent champion of Women's Lib.

"Put your suitcase on the bed," she told him. "You'll find a place for your things in the wardrobe over there. As soon as you've unpacked, I'll have Jose bring in a tray with your dinner."

Bloom shook his head. "That won't be necessary. I had a very late lunch. If you don't mind, I'd just like to rest for a little while."

"Suit yourself." Miss Cox turned, moving toward the doorway. She halted there and glanced back. "I do hope you'll be comfortable here. If you want to wash up, there's a towel and a washcloth on the shelf in your wardrobe locker. The men's bathroom is at the end of the hall. Now I'd better be getting back to my desk. If there's anything else you need, let me know."

Before he could reply, she exited quickly, leaving him alone in the room.

Mr. Bloom surveyed it with a rueful smile. *Welcome to Sunneyvale*.

His glance traveled across the narrow beds, each covered by a drab gray blanket; the exposed borders of the sheets and the single pillow were white, but they too had a grayish tinge, the product of too many washings and too little bleach. The late afternoon sun shown dimly through windows at the far end of the room, but its rays were not strong enough to dispel the shadows blurring the outline of the shelves above each bed, the woodened-back chair beside it, or the wardrobe cabinets on the opposite wall.

Everything seemed gray here, including the inmates.

Guests, Mr. Bloom corrected himself. All the residents were paying guests, courtesy of Social Security, Medicare, pensions, and savings. And as long as they paid, they stayed; stayed in their gray dormitory until a deeper darkness descended—the darkness of death. Sunneyvale was no different from the other retirement homes he'd seen; just another warehouse for senior citizens awaiting graduation into oblivion.

Bloom shrugged, then picked up his suitcase and carried it, unopened, to the wardrobe locker. Stooping, he set it down inside, then straightened and squared his shoulders. It was time to go.

The sun was already starting to disappear over the horizon beyond the wide picture windows as Bloom entered the recreation room.

Apparently both the football game and the dinner hour were over, because Mrs. Dempsey and Mrs. Weinstein were seated with the three men on the chairs and settee grouped before the television set. On-screen, an elderly gentleman with a shock of curly hair the color of cotton candy was grinning out at his unseen audience.

"Let me run through that again," his vibrant voice resounded through the room. "Vitamin A for your scalp, vision, and teeth. Vitamin B for hair and healthy mucous membranes. Vitamin C for the teeth and circulatory system. Remember, C will help keep those lips from shrinking."

Bloom glanced at the men. One was tall and thin, wearing scholarly horn-rims and a most unscholarly bathrobe; Bloom took a quick guess, deciding that he would be Mr. Mute, perhaps because his mouth was so tightly closed as he stared in stoic skepticism at the screen.

The one seated on the settee beside Mrs. Weinstein must be her husband, so the gentleman in the chair next to Mrs. Dempsey had to be Mr. Agee. At first glance he appeared to be quite handsome and well-preserved for his age; evidently he must have taken a good share of every vitamin in alphabetical order.

But Mr. Weinstein seemed to have neglected his ABCs. He was a bald-headed little man in his early eighties, his face shriveled, thin lips pursed in permanent disapproval of everything his long nose sniffed or his melancholy eyes surveyed.

Now those eyes glanced up at the newcomer, and the lips parted as Mr. Weinstein rose, nodding. "You must be Mr. Bloom, right?"

Bloom nodded. "And you are—?"

"Weinstein." The bald-headed man gestured toward his seated companion. "This is my wife, Mrs. Winston."

"Winston?" Bloom cast a puzzled glance as the plump woman in the dark wig rose and extended her hand in greeting.

"Weinstein," she said. "Sadie Weinstein." She smiled. "Don't pay any attention to that husband of mine, Mr. Bloom. Our son Murray, he changed his name to Winston and my husband doesn't approve."

"What's to approve?" Mr. Weinstein shook his head. "Just because he goes into politics he thinks he has to change his name to get ahead."

"And why not?" his wife challenged. "You think maybe people in England would vote for somebody named Weinstein Churchill?"

"Don't pay any attention to her." Mr. Weinstein reached out and patted the plump arm of his spouse. "My wife is a closet *goy*."

The other members of the group had risen; stepping forward, they introduced themselves in turn.

"Welcome aboard," Mr. Agee said, his hand-clasp firm.

"So nice to have you with us." Mrs. Dempsey fanned his face with a flutter of false eyelashes. "I hope you'll like it here."

"Pleased to meet you, Mr. Bloom." A look of inquiry flashed from behind Mr. Mute's horn-rims. "Your first name doesn't happen to be Leopold, by any chance?"

Bloom smiled. "I'm afraid I can't lay claim to such distinction," he said. "I never had the privilege of meeting James Joyce, and I'm not a native of Dublin."

"You're from Minneapolis, aren't you?" Mrs. Weinstein said. "I heard Miss Cox talking with you on the phone the other day—"

"You got big ears." Her husband frowned his disapproval. "And Miss Cox has a big mouth." He turned to Bloom and nodded. "Sit down, make yourself comfortable."

"Thank you." Bloom smiled, glancing toward the picture windows. "I'll join you in a moment. If you don't mind, right now I'd rather watch the sunset instead of television."

"Feel free," Mr. Mute told him. "Personally, I'd prefer to curl up with a good book—or a bad woman. Unfortunately, both seem to be in short supply around here."

As he settled back down into his seat, the others followed suit, their eyes automatically returning to focus on the tube. The man with the cotton-candy hair was offering more words of wisdom to the world.

"And let's not forget E, the miracle vitamin. If you've enjoyed a healthy sex life, there's no reason why you can't keep on well into your golden years, thanks to a daily intake of Vitamin E . . ."

Golden years. Bloom moved to the nearest window, staring out into the sunset. It too was golden, but now its luster faded into gray gloom.

In the street beyond, a group of children were playing a game of kick-the-can, laughing and shouting in the gathering twilight. Bloom smiled appreciatively at the sight. The childhood years —these were truly golden.

Now his attention shifted to the driveway before the rest home's entrance. Here another group stood before a parked car—a stout, bearded man in his middle thirties, a blond woman around the same age, and an elderly gentleman who clutched a cardboard suitcase in one hand. Remembering what Miss Cox had told him, Bloom guessed the identities of the trio—Mr. Conroy, his son, and his daughter-in-law. He couldn't hear their conversation through the window but pantomime and body language offered an eloquence of their own. *One picture is worth a thousand words—*

The bulk of those words issued from Mr.

Conroy's contorted mouth; words that pleaded, words that begged; and the suitcase told its own story.

"Take me home with you," the mouth implored. "Let me come just for the weekend" was the message of the small suitcase. "I promise I won't be in your way—"

The frown on the bearded face and the repeated shaking of the head adorned with brassy blond curls also translated easily into words: "Sorry, Pop. Not this time. We're all tied up for tonight and tomorrow we promised to take the kids to the beach."

The daughter-in-law glanced at her watch, then looked up with a frown. It didn't require any talent in lip-reading to know what she was saying. "Look at the time, Joe! We really have to leave now."

Mr. Conroy stepped back, shoulders sagging in surrender as his son and daughter-in-law settled themselves comfortably in the bucket seats of the shiny new Cadillac and closed the door with a big-car bang. His son started the engine, then pressed a button to roll down the automatic window and flash a smile of surpassing warmth and phoniness at his father. Again Bloom put words into the moving mouth: "Maybe next week, Pop. Okay?"

The car glided down the driveway, turned left, then vanished from view. Mr. Conroy stood motionless for a moment, his eyes following its progress until he could see it no longer. The shadows gathering around the driveway were gray; second childhood has no golden years.

"Poor Leo!" Bloom started at the sound of the

voice behind him. Turning, he saw Mr. Agee standing at his elbow, shaking his head.

"Every Saturday, Leo carries that suitcase out to his kid's car and every Saturday he carries it back again and unpacks."

"Don't they ever let him come to visit?"

"Maybe once or twice a year, over the holidays. They do a lot of partying and entertaining—mostly for business, you know. His son's in real estate."

Mr. Bloom nodded. "I guessed as much when I saw him smile."

Mr. Agee chuckled. "You've got quite a sense of humor, Mr. Bloom."

Bloom didn't reply; he was still staring out of the window, watching as the old man with a suitcase turned and started back up the driveway. As he did so, his shuffling feet encountered the tin can that the children were using in their game. For some reason it had been placed at the edge of the drive and now a small girl was running toward it hastily, ready to kick the can and be "safe" according to the rules of the game.

Either Mr. Conroy didn't see her coming or else he didn't give a damn. Noticing the can before him, he lashed out with his foot and sent it sailing across the lawn. Then he resumed his plodding progress up the drive.

Behind him the little girl grimaced in exasperation, then turned and ran toward the rolling can as a boy—obviously "it" in the game—emerged from the street to follow her in hot pursuit.

Reaching the rolling can, the girl kicked it with

all her might, her mouth opening in a silent shout, which Bloom promptly mimicked.

"Alley-alley-oxen-free!"

All eyes turned from the television screen now and Bloom greeted their stares with a smile. "Sorry, I didn't mean to interrupt your program. I was just watching the kids outside—guess I must have let myself get carried away."

"Don't apologize," said Mr. Weinstein. "The kind of programs they got on tonight we can do without, believe me. 'Saturday Night Live,' 'Saturday Night Dead'—who needs it?"

Now there was another interruption in the form—two forms, really—of Mr. Conroy and Miss Cox, as they entered the room together, halting just inside the doorway.

Seeing the latest arrival standing at the window, Miss Cox called out to him. "Having fun, Mr. Bloom? Why don't you come over here for a moment. I'd like to introduce you to one of your roommates."

Bloom nodded and crossed toward her, wondering as he did so just how much fun Miss Cox imagined he might enjoy just by looking out the window. Perhaps she mistook him for a voyeur. And he hardly regarded the other male residents as roommates; the term would be more appropriate if applied to the youngsters in a boarding school. Unless, of course, Miss Cox was recycling it to do service in his second childhood.

Abruptly he put his thoughts aside to acknowledge her introduction.

"Mr. Conroy, this is Mr. Bloom, our new resident."

"Pleased to meet you," Mr. Conroy said. His attempt at a smile was not too successful, nor was his effort to shake hands, for as he raised his arm he realized that he was still clutching his suitcase by the handle.

"Here, let me take that." Miss Cox snatched the suitcase from his grasp. "I'll put it away for you. Why don't you just stay here now and get acquainted with our new arrival?"

She nodded at Bloom. "Mr. Conroy's first name is Leo," she told him, then paused, frowning slightly. "I'm sorry, but I can't seem to recall yours."

"Don't be sorry." Bloom smiled at her. "I haven't given you my first name."

"But I must have—"

Miss Cox broke off as the ring of a phone echoed from the hall. With a frown she hurried out, carrying Mr. Conroy's suitcase with her.

Bloom found himself surrounded by smiling faces.

"Good on you," Mr. Weinstein said. "That's telling her!"

The others nodded approvingly; only Mr. Conroy seemed upset and his scowl of irritation was directed at the picture window facing the street beyond. He moved toward it, peering out into the dusk.

"Damn kids," he muttered. "They've been told not to play around here. Old people need their rest."

Mrs. Dempsey spoke up. "But we can't even *hear*

them, Mr. Conroy! Let the youngsters have their fun. I only wish I could go out there and play with them myself."

Bloom nodded. "Why don't you, Mrs. Dempsey?" he said softly.

She started to laugh, then broke off as Leo Conroy answered for her. "Because she's old, Mr. Bloom."

Bloom shook his head. "I don't think we're ever too old to play. When you rest, you rust."

A fluffy white pillow suddenly uncoiled on the arm of the chair where Mrs. Dempsey had been sitting. Bloom blinked, then recognized her cat.

Mrs. Dempsey went to pick it up. As she cradled it in her arms, the cat began to purr, and so did Mrs. Dempsey. "What's the matter, Mickey? Don't you like television?"

"What's to like?" Mr. Weinstein cast a sour glance at the screen, as a grinning, hyperactive game-show host fired an inane question at an equally inane contestant. "Why don't we turn it off? All this racket makes it so a fella can't think. I'd like a chance to get acquainted with Mr. Bloom here."

"Good idea." Mrs. Weinstein nodded approvingly at her spouse. "It's been a long time since I had a chance to *schmooz* with anybody new."

"Excellent!" said Mr. Mute. "The trouble with all these game-shows is that nobody loses except the viewers."

He moved to the set and switched it off.

As the tube went blank, the others took their

seats again. Bloom followed Mr. Conroy to the far end of the semicircle of chairs and sat down between him and Mrs. Dempsey.

Mr. Conroy turned to him. "Is this your first time in an old-age home, Bloom?"

Bloom shook his head, conscious that everyone was waiting for an answer. "No. Actually, Mr. Conroy, I've been in six or eight of them."

"Six or eight homes?" Mr. Conroy raised his bushy eyebrows. "That's quite a record, Bloom. What's your problem—can't make any friends?"

Mrs. Dempsey produced a sniff of indignation. "I think Mr. Bloom is a *very* friendly person! Which is more than I can say for some people around here."

Bloom smiled at her. "Tell me, Mrs. Dempsey. If you could go out there with those children tonight, what would you want to play?"

Mrs. Dempsey stroked her cat. "I used to love all kinds of games. Especially jacks. I was the jacks champion in elementary school," she announced proudly.

"Those were the good old days," said Mr. Mute. "Kids don't play jacks anymore. Now they're only interested in jocks."

Mrs. Dempsey uttered a surprisingly girlish giggle. "But you know, if I could still tell my body what to do, I would dance."

Mr. Agee rose and crossed to her, extending his hand. "I would be honored to have this dance, Mrs. Dempsey."

Mrs. Dempsey giggled again and started to rise,

then winced in sudden pain and slumped back again.

"What's the matter?" Mr. Agee bent over her solicitously.

"Just a shooting pain." Mrs. Dempsey shook her head, embarrassed. "I think it's my arthuritis."

"Arthritis," Mr. Weinstein corrected. "Since when do you go around calling diseases by their first name?"

Everyone laughed—everyone except Mr. Conroy. "Speak for yourself," he said. "When you've got as many aches and pains as I have, you get to know them personally."

"Don't remind me." Mrs. Weinstein glanced at Bloom. "I would like to run again. What I wouldn't give to play jump rope once more."

Mr. Agee nodded. "What I wouldn't give to just be hitting puberty again!"

"Sex!" Mr. Conroy muttered. "Is that all you ever think about?"

"So what's wrong with thinking?" Mrs. Weinstein reached out and took her husband's hand. "Maybe that's one game I can't play anymore, but believe me, I've got some beautiful memories."

"Stop already." Mr. Weinstein squeezed her hand. "You've had a full life, sweetheart. Don't get sloppy on me now." Glancing down, he noticed his wife's shoes resting beside the settee and pointed at them. "Put those back on. A good Jew only goes barefoot when someone has died."

Mrs. Weinstein shrugged. "I'm not that orthodox."

"I am," Mr. Weinstein said firmly. "Put 'em on before you catch cold."

Bloom leaned forward to address him. "What were you like as a boy, Mr. Weinstein?"

"Me?" Mr. Weinstein smiled. "I loved to climb —anything you can name, I climbed it. Like a cat I could climb."

Mr. Agee chimed in, nodding. "I always wanted to be Douglas Fairbanks."

"You still do, Mr. Agee." Mrs. Dempsey giggled again.

"Did you know Douglas Fairbanks was half Jewish?" Mr. Weinstein said. "His real name was Ullman."

Mr. Agee ignored him, lost in the depth of fond recollection. "I broke more bedsprings by leaping from my dresser to the bed and out the window."

Again there was laughter from the group and again Mr. Conroy abstained. It was obvious he had no intention of joining them in this stroll down Memory Lane.

"Have it your way," he said. "Me, I *like* being old." He stared at the group defiantly. "And when I go, my son promised to have me frozen."

"You already are frozen, popsicle-head!" Mr. Weinstein declared. He started to laugh at his own joke, then began to cough. Mrs. Weinstein slapped him on the back.

"Watch it, Harry," she chided. "Remember your emphysema."

"She's right." Mr. Conroy nodded grimly. "Face the facts. We'd all be better off if we remember

what we are today, instead of what happened sixty
—seventy years ago."

But Mrs. Dempsey ignored him. As the coughing
spell ended, she glanced at Bloom. "What about
you?" she asked. "What did you play?"

Bloom smiled. "Kick-the-can was my game."

"That was mostly for boys," Mrs. Dempsey said.
"My late husband, Jack Dempsey—not the fighter,
Mr. Bloom—Jack Dempsey was the most gentle man
who ever walked this earth—he loved that game."

Mr. Conroy fidgeted in his chair. "What's the point
of all this talk? Why are you dredging up the past,
Bloom? This isn't healthy."

But Mrs. Dempsey ignored him. "Like I was
saying, Mr. Bloom, he just loved that game. His
mother would bean him if she caught him playing.
Ruined his shoes, she said."

"Marbles." Mr. Weinstein nodded, taking a ride on
his own train of recollections. "There was a game for
you!"

"Do you still remember what those marbles were
called?" Mr. Agee asked.

Mr. Weinstein gestured quickly. "Don't say it
—I'm thinking. Agates. Purees. And laggars—"

Mrs. Dempsey sighed. "It was so nice, being a
child. There was nothing to worry about because
people always took care of me."

"They take care of you here." Mr. Conroy offered a
smile dipped in vinegar. "Miss Cox takes great care of
you, doesn't let you do a thing."

Mrs. Dempsey wasn't listening. "I had lots of
friends and ever so many toys—"

"Toys?" Mr. Conroy's voice rose, insistent upon her attention. "They've got toys here that will last you for the rest of your life. Oxygen tanks, respirators, bedpans, the whole works." There was vinegar in his voice now. "You want friends? Mr. Bloom here is trying to make friends—trying to stir them all up, aren't you, Bloom?"

Frowning, Mr. Mute attempted a diversion. He leaned forward quickly, addressing Mr. Weinstein. "What were the clay marbles called, Harry?"

For a moment Mr. Weinstein sat silent. So did the others, as the impact of Mr. Conroy's words hit home.

Mr. Agee tried again. "Well, Harry?"

Mr. Weinstein shrugged his shoulders and expelled a sigh of misery. "I don't know. I can't remember anymore."

Bloom leaned forward. "Sure you can, " he said. "The clays ones were emis."

"That's right." Mr. Weinstein looked up, nodding gratefully. "Emis. Now I remember!" He smiled. "Thank you, Bloom, you're a real *mensch.*"

Bloom glanced thoughtfully at the semicircle of faces, capturing their attention as he spoke. "The day we stopped playing is the day we started getting old. We started watching clocks, watching for the days to hurry up and end, counting weeks and months and years as if they would last forever. We never realized our time would run out, and that's where we made our mistake."

He nodded slowly. "We never should have

started counting, never been in such a hurry to grow up, because once the counting begins, it never stops. The clock keeps right on going, ticking your life away. But when we played, we weren't worried about time. We always had something else to look forward to—another chance to hide, another turn at bat, another game of kick-the-can—"

He halted, eyes searching their faces in the silence. "So who's playing?"

Mr. Weinstein blinked at him, startled. "What?"

Bloom smiled. "I'm starting up a game of kick-the-can! Who's playing?"

Mr. Conroy shook his head. "When's the last time you fell down and couldn't get up by yourself, pal? How dare you ask anybody to go out there and risk the little bit of life they have left in them!"

"All life is a risk, Mr. Conroy. I'm not asking anybody to do what I'm not willing to do. But maybe if we played, we might get a hold on that thing we're all missing—a little hold on youth."

Mr. Conroy gestured contemptuously toward his companions. "Look at them," he muttered. "Their bones will break if they try to run. Their hearts are old. Their lungs are old."

Mrs. Dempsey glanced up timidly. "Miss Cox would *never* allow us to go outside and play, Mr. Bloom. It's against the rules."

"Rules!" Mr. Bloom shook his head. "Did you ever try to stop a child? Are you going to let rules stop you from the chance of being young again?"

Now Bloom reached into his jacket pocket. When it emerged he was holding an object that brought startled gasps from the semicircle.

Resting against the palm of his hand was a tin can.

Ignoring their stares, ignoring their exclamations of surprise, he reached into his pocket again. Pulling out a handkerchief he began to polish the surface of the empty can.

It was only then that he glanced up, nodding. "This old man still has a little magic left in him. If you believe, I think I can promise to make you feel like children again."

Mr. Conroy snickered. "You're making promises that they can't keep, Bloom."

Bloom didn't reply; he was already turning to the others. "I want to see you dance, Mrs. Dempsey. And you, Mr. Weinstein—how would you like to be able to climb again?"

Mr. Weinstein nodded. "Like a cat I could climb."

Bloom rose. "Let's break the rules. What can they take away from us that we haven't already lost?"

As his challenge echoed, it was greeted with a quick exchange of glances, followed by a hushed, expectant silence.

"Well, what do you say?" Mr. Bloom nodded. "Don't waste time, or time will waste you."

Mr. Agee cleared his throat. "When were you thinking of playing?" he asked.

Bloom held up the tin can, its polished surface gleaming beneath the light.

"Tonight," he said.

Again the exchange of glances—again the hush of anticipation.

Mr. Weinstein glanced toward the window; the street beyond was almost invisible in the darkness. "You mean right now?" He shook his head sadly. "God forbid Miss Cox should see us, she'll lock us up and throw the key away."

"That's not the game plan," Bloom told him. "What I suggest is that we all go to bed until midnight. Then, after we make sure Miss Cox is sound asleep, we can tiptoe out—"

"Marvelous!" Mrs. Weinstein clapped her hands.

Mr. Mute was nodding. "I agree! Just thinking about it is enough to bring on my formication!"

"Watch your language!" Mr. Weinstein shook his finger. "I don't like anybody talking dirty in front of my wife!"

Behind his horn-rims, Mr. Mute's eyes sparkled with amusement. "Not fornication," he said. "For*m*ication, with an *m*. It refers to having a feeling that ants are crawling under your skin." He laughed happily. "Got you that time, didn't I, Harry!"

Mr. Weinstein shook his head. "Remember what it says in the Talmud," he murmured. "Nobody loves a smart-ass."

Now he turned, joining his wife, Mrs. Dempsey, and Mr. Agee as they stood clustered before Bloom.

There was an almost palpable excitement radiating through the room. Mr. Mute stepped up behind him, reaching out to touch the tin can with tingling fingers.

"You're not putting us on, Mr. Bloom?" he said. "Do you really think we can get away with it without being caught?"

"Not a chance!"

Mr. Conroy's voice was scornful. He sat stubbornly in his chair, shaking his head as they turned to stare at him. "I've got five bucks that says none of you old crocks can still keep your eyes open after ten o'clock!"

Bloom smiled. "Don't worry about that—I'm a regular night owl." He turned his attention to the group before him. "Why don't you all try to sleep for a few hours? When the time comes, I'll drop around and let you know."

Mr. Conroy grunted. "Don't bother to wake me up," he said. "I may be old, but I'm not senile enough to crawl out of bed in the middle of the night just to play some damn-fool kid's game."

For a moment the group's decision wavered in the balance. Then Mr. Mute nodded at Bloom. "See you later," he said. Turning, he gestured to his fellow resident.

"Let's go," he murmured. "It's time for all of us damn fools to get some rest before the game."

Mr. Conroy sat alone in the recreation room, watching the ten o'clock news. He always watched the news before going to bed and he was damned if he'd miss it now just because of this nonsense tonight.

He still didn't understand how the others could fall for such foolishness. They ought to act their age. If those idiots thought that playing some kid's game at midnight would make them feel young again, then maybe they'd have to learn the hard way. Nobody can turn the clock back. It was just wishful thinking. They wanted youth, but all they would get out of this was a broken hip, a stroke, maybe a heart attack.

The whole idea was crazy. They must be crazy, too—listening to somebody like Bloom—because he was the craziest of them all.

For a moment he wondered if he ought to inform Miss Cox that she was harboring a lunatic under her roof. Then he dismissed the notion with a shrug. Why should he do her any favors? Let her find out the hard way, too. What anyone else did was their business.

His business was to watch the news so that he could be sure of getting a good night's sleep. Other people counted sheep, but Mr. Conroy had found a method of his own. He watched the news and kept count of the day's events.

Listening to the commentator, he made a tally on his mental score-card: three murders . . . two rapes . . . six muggings . . . one armed robbery . . . one tornado, one explosion, several floods and famines . . . three fires, two of which were obviously arson . . . plus, as a final bonus, four wars and a revolutionary uprising.

Not bad for one evening; just thinking about what went on in the outside world was enough to make you welcome sleep.

Satisfied, Mr. Conroy rose, switched off the television, and shuffled down the hall.

When he reached the dormitory, he was greeted by the snores of his fellow residents. Quietly, he undressed in darkness so as not to disturb them. The only sound rising above the even snores was a faint plop as he dropped his teeth into a glass of water on the shelf above his bed. Then he scrunched down beneath the covers and in a matter of moments his own snore joined the chorus.

It had not been easy for Mr. Weinstein to fall asleep. Usually he went out like a light the moment his head touched the pillow, but tonight was different. So much had happened and there was so much to think about.

Of course, this fella Bloom was a *meshuganah*, but it didn't matter. Not for one minute could Mr. Weinstein believe that climbing out of his nice warm bed to play kick-the-can in the middle of the night was going to make anyone feel young again; for people his age the Fountain of Youth had been turned off long ago. But at least he was willing to go along with the idea, if only to break the monotony. Maybe Bloom was a genuine eighteen-carat nutzo, but at least he was bringing them a little action, giving them something new to think about, opening the windows and letting in a little fresh air.

So what if Bloom couldn't really make them young again? Maybe just doing something different would make them *feel* younger for a little while, help take away the boredom.

That was the worst part of getting old, Mr. Weinstein decided. You got used to being bored, used to just sitting on your *tochus* all day while the world changed. After a while you didn't even notice the changes anymore; then all of a sudden you looked around and everything was different. Now all the boys were named David and all the girls were Jennifers.

But one thing didn't change: kids still had their youth, their strength, their health; and Mr. Weinstein envied them for that. As for him, all he had was a bad heart—and poor Sadie, complaining about her back pains. *Funny; everybody seems to complain about back pains and nobody even mentions front pains. Go figure that one out.* Mr. Weinstein was still figuring as he fell asleep.

In the women's dormitory, Mrs. Dempsey was already sleeping with Mickey curled up beside her pillow. In her dream the white cat suddenly turned into her husband Jack, and Mrs. Dempsey wasted no time. They began to make love. Somewhere along the line Jack Dempsey turned into Clark Gable, but Mrs. Dempsey didn't mind. She went right on making love. . . .

Mr. Agee wasn't dreaming about a movie star in his dream. He *was* the star himself. A handsome, dashing Douglas Fairbanks, he slashed a villain's face with the Z of Zorro, crossed swords with the Three Musketeers, rode the magic carpet over Baghdad, and swung through the trees of Sherwood Forest with all the ease and grace of Robin Hood. . . .

*   *   *

Mrs. Weinstein stirred restlessly. If Miss Cox would only give her a room of her own where she and Harry could sleep in the same bed, maybe things would be different. Not that there would be any fooling around—nobody fools around at her age, no matter how many vitamins they take. But at least the two of them could be together, just like they had been for all those years before.

No, suppose Harry *were* here—what difference would it make? They probably wouldn't even talk; the way she felt now, all she wanted to do was sleep. Face wooden, limbs stiff, Mrs. Weinstein slept like a log.

Mr. Mute fell asleep thinking about mole rats. Somewhere recently he'd run across a reference to these curious creatures, either in his reading or else while watching one of those nature documentaries on television. And now, strangely enough, they came scampering through his thoughts, burrowing into his brain the way they burrowed through the sun-baked earth below the savanna grasslands of East Africa. There, in the warm darkness, they nestled in a tangled drove, venturing forth only to bring food into the pitch-black confines where they lived out their entire existence in half-blind hunger. Here they mated in a crawling mass, cleansing the bodies of the newborn with their urine, feeding on their own excrement and redigesting it, spending their lives in squalor, away from the sunshine of the world outside.

Miserable creatures, leading a miserable life. But just how different was it from his own existence here at Sunneyvale? Crowded together in the confines of the so-called recreation room, sitting and staring half-blindly at the television tube, redigesting memories of the past, shut away from the world beyond?

Mr. Mute was still pondering the question as, like a mole rat, he burrowed down into the darkness of slumber.

Miss Cox was asleep, too. Bloom looked in on her for a moment, gently easing open the door of the bedroom at the far end of the hall. The bedside lamp was still burning; she must have dozed off while reading, for a paperback romance rested beside her, its gaudy cover-art displaying the standard frightened heroine fleeing from the conventional Gothic mansion with the inevitable dark-haired and mustachioed hero staring after her.

Such stuff as dreams are made of. Bloom smiled and closed the door. Then he turned and walked softly down the hall.

It was exactly midnight when he entered the men's dormitory and moved in semidarkness to Mr. Mute's bedside. Bending down, he shook him gently by the shoulder.

"It's time, Mr. Mute," he whispered.

Mr. Mute opened his eyes and sat up, throwing back his covers. He was fully clothed; the discarded bathrobe rested on the chair beside him.

Bloom stared at him approvingly. "I see you're

dressed for the occasion," he murmured. "What about the others?"

Mr. Mute nodded. "They all went to bed with their clothes on, at my suggestion." He glanced toward the sleeping forms in the beds beside him. "All but Conroy. He must have come in later, but I see he's wearing his pajamas."

"Try not to disturb him," Bloom said. "Now, if you'll just wake the others, I'll go down the hall and see if the ladies are ready. We'll meet outside on the back lawn. I've been scouting around for a good place and that seems to be the safest."

"Excellent." Mr. Mute reached for his glasses on the shelf above the bed. "See you in a few minutes."

When Bloom stepped out onto the back lawn, he found the others already waiting. Carrying the tin can, he moved to the center of the greensward, beckoning the others to follow him.

"All set?" he asked.

"Ready to go." Mr. Agee winked at Mrs. Dempsey.

She nodded, cradling the cat against her shoulder.

Mr. Weinstein shrugged. "I feel like a *schlemiel*," he murmured. "But what have I got to lose?"

"Right," said Bloom. "Here we go." He tossed the can into the air.

As it whirled down in a shimmering spiral the old people ran for cover, finding hiding-places in the hedge and shrubbery that bordered the lawn on three sides.

Bloom stared down at the can; then, in a loud voice, he slowly counted to ten.

Turning, he moved over the bordering hedge at his right and began to search for the other players.

Behind his back they were already sneaking forward one by one, emerging from their various hiding places to kick the can.

When Bloom looked toward the center of the lawn again, he was greeted with giggles and laughter.

"Fooled you this time!" Mrs. Dempsey cried.

"So you did." Bloom nodded. "Looks like I'm it again."

He tossed the can. The old folks ran. Bloom counted, and above him the full moon turned the night to silver.

In the dormitory, Mr. Conroy tossed and turned restlessly. Through his slumber the voices of the old people on the lawn filtered faintly. But as their play continued, the sound of their shouts and laughters began to change. Now the shrill tones echoed like the voices of children. *"Alley-alley-oxen-free!"* someone shouted.

"Damn kids—" Mumbling in his sleep, Mr. Conroy buried his head beneath the pillow.

On the lawn under the full moon, a small red-haired boy pranced joyfully, flapping the sleeves and trouser bottoms of Mr. Mute's suit.

"Kids!" he cried.

And kids they were—each and every one of them. Laughing children, clad in the outsized outfits of Harry and Sadie Weinstein, Mr. Agee, and Mrs. Dempsey. Mrs. Dempsey was still holding her cat, but it was a kitten now.

Mr. Weinstein glanced at the cute little girl beside him. "Sadie?"

She nodded in delight. "Is that you, Harry?" Reaching out, she gave his cheek a pinch. "Such a little *maeskite!*"

Young Mr. Mute clapped his hands exuberantly. "Kids!" he shouted again. "Look at us—it's really happened!"

Rolling up his trouser bottoms, a boyish Mr. Agee glanced toward Bloom, who had seated himself on a bench near the back door.

"Mr. Bloom—are you all right?"

Bloom nodded. "Certainly."

Little Mrs. Dempsey turned and stared. "But you're still old!"

"Am I? I never thought of it that way." He gestured. "Don't worry about me—just enjoy yourselves."

Mr. Weinstein glanced down and shook his head. *"Oy gevalt,* look how short I am!"

"Never mind," Bloom told him. "You want to play, you have to keep playing."

And play they did, fulfilling the fantasies of youth under the full moon.

Mrs. Weinstein and Mrs. Dempsey danced together, two doll-like figures twirling in the moonlight.

Mr. Agee began a fencing match with an imaginary opponent. Forcing his invincible foe back, he leaped onto the bench on which Bloom was sitting, giving him just enough time to rise before the bench tipped over. Landing on his feet with Fairbanksian grace, he continued his sword fight until he reached the dancing girls. Halting his duel, he winked at Mrs. Dempsey. "Dance with me!" he cried.

Mrs. Dempsey moved into his arms immediately. He grabbed her close and tried to kiss her.

She struggled free shaking her head. "Oh, no, Mr. Agee—stay away from me!"

"Okay." Mr. Agee grinned, then turned and reached out to embrace Mrs. Weinstein.

"No!" She shook her head. "Dirty old man!"

"Not anymore!" Mr. Agee lunged for her again. Still resisting, she turned and called over her shoulder. "Harry! Where are you?"

Mr. Weinstein swung into view from the overhanging limb of a tall tree, dangling by one arm. He shouted, "Agee, get away from my wife!"

As Agee released her, Mrs. Weinstein turned and glanced anxiously at her husband. "Harry—your heart—"

Mr. Weinstein laughed. "My heart? Are you kidding?" Swinging from the limb, he let out a Tarzan yell.

Clothes flying, little Mr. Mute somersaulted across the lawn and came to a stop at Bloom's feet. At the same moment Mr. Agee leaped to a halt beside him.

"Look," he said. "I don't wish to appear ungrateful, but why don't you join us?"

Bloom shrugged. "I find I prefer to be my true age and try to keep my mind young." His nod included the others as they approached. "But your wish has come true. You're children again. You have your whole lives before you."

A most unboyish frown creased Mr. Mute's forehead. "My life was so hard," he murmured.

"I had a swell life," Mr. Agee said. "I can do sixty years more standing on my head."

"So who wants to live upside down?" Mr. Weinstein smiled. "Me, I was just beginning to look forward to senility."

His wife shivered in the breeze rising from beyond the hedge. "I'm cold. Where are we going to spend the night? Where can we go? Who'll take care of us?"

Mr. Weinstein put his arms around her. "No problem," he said. "We'll just knock on our son's door and say, 'Let us in, Murray, we're your parents.' Don't worry—you know how he loves kids."

Mrs. Weinstein sighed. "I love you, Harry, but I don't want to go back and do it all over again."

"Now wait a minute," Mr. Agee said. "Let's think this over. There's a lot to look forward to. I'm talking about sex—"

Mrs. Dempsey was dismayed. "Jack Dempsey isn't here. I'll never meet him—" As she spoke, she glanced down at her hand. Then cried out, "My ring! My wedding ring. It fell off!"

Dropping to her knees, she began to search the lawn. The others came to her aid.

Hands scrabbling desperately through the grass, Mrs. Dempsey shook her head. "I didn't really ask to be young again, all I wanted to do was dance! I can be old and dance."

Beside her Mr. Mute nodded. "I'm *not* going to school again," he declared.

"School is easy," Mr. Weinstein said. "But work another forty years? Forget it!" Now he noticed that his wife was barefooted again. Pointing at oversized shoes lying discarded near the bench, he issued his orders. "Put 'em on. Nobody died here!"

Mrs. Weinstein obeyed, but the mention of death brought a look of sadness to her girlish face. "I don't want to lose the people I love again, one by one. I remember the night my father passed away. They laid him out and then they sent all us children outside. We saw Halley's Comet."

"I was too young to see Halley's Comet," Mrs. Dempsey told her. "I was going to see it when I was eighty years old."

Bloom spoke gently. "That's only two more birthdays, Mrs. Dempsey. Would you like to see it at eight, or at eighty?"

Mrs. Dempsey reached down and lifted her kitten from the lawn. "Eighty," she murmured.

Bloom nodded, then extended his hand. "Look —I seem to have found your ring."

Smiling gratefully, Mrs. Dempsey slid the large loop onto a small finger. "I'll still have this," she said, "and all the memories that go with it."

"Me too," said Mrs. Weinstein. "In spite of everything, I'm satisfied with my life the way it was. We should take one day at a time."

"I agree," her husband said. "What we got to do is try to make those days a little better."

Bloom smiled. "In that case, let's all go back to bed. Maybe you could wake up in your old bodies again, but with fresh young minds."

Picking up the tin can, he moved to the back door and the group trailed after him—children following the Pied Piper.

Only Mr. Agee seemed reluctant. "Can't we discuss it? I'm not tired yet!"

"You can't go on like this forever," said Mr. Weinstein. "It's fun for a while, but who wants to spend the rest of their lives playing kick-the-can?"

Bloom opened the door and gestured. "In you go," he whispered. "And remember—no noise."

They stepped past him into the hall one by one, tiptoeing quietly. Mr. Mute brought up the rear and as he reached the doorway he paused and glanced up at the tin can Bloom was holding in his hand. "One question," he murmured. "I still don't see how you did it. Is there some kind of magical property in that can?"

"Not really." Bloom tossed the can away, sailing it through the moonlight to land in the shadows beyond. He smiled.

"The magic is in yourselves."

Mr. Conroy was still asleep when his fellow residents moved into the dormitory. It was only the whispering in the hall outside that awakened him.

"But I'm not ready to go back. I want to stay like this!"

Conroy didn't identify Mr. Agee's childish treble, but he recognized Bloom as he replied. "That's up to you. Are you quite sure—?"

"Positive."

"So be it, then," said Bloom. "But you'd better get back into bed anyway, before somebody sees you here in the hall."

It was then that Mr. Conroy opened his eyes, just in time to see Bloom enter, followed by little Mr. Agee. The sight of the child in his oversized garments was enough to bring Mr. Conroy bolt-upright against the back of his bed. Turning, he glanced along the row at the diminutive heads of Mr. Mute and Mr. Weinstein already nestling on their pillows.

"Jesus H. Christ!" said Mr. Conroy.

Ignoring the restraining wave of Bloom's hand, he jumped out of bed and raced out into the hall.

The door to the men's dormitory was closed when Mr. Conroy returned. Miss Cox, clad in a frilly negligee, stumbled behind him.

"It wasn't a dream—I saw them!" Mr. Conroy's voice echoed through the corridor. "Kids! Kids in the beds!"

Miss Cox shook her head in disbelief until her curlers rattled. Sighing, she opened the door and peered inside.

Mr. Mute, Mr. Weinstein, and Bloom lay sound asleep, their lined, familiar faces pressed against the pillows. Mr. Agee's bed was also occupied, although he'd pulled the covers up over his head.

Now Mr. Conroy quailed before Miss Cox's accusing stare.

"But they *were* kids!" he faltered.

"You had a nightmare." Miss Cox's voice softened into weary resignation as she took the old man by his arm. "Come on, back to bed with you."

She led Mr. Conroy into the room, and it was then that Mr. Agee's bed erupted.

With a whirl of scattering blankets, young Mr. Agee bounded upward. Using the bed as a trampoline, he bounced up and down upon it, then jumped to the windowsill in a leap that would have made Douglas Fairbanks proud of him.

Raising the window, he turned and nodded at Miss Cox.

"Welcome to Sherwood Forest, m'lady!" He grinned at Mr. Conroy. "How now, Sir Guy, no greetings from you?"

Mr. Conroy stared in shock, but Miss Cox's anger found a voice. "What are you doing in here, you little ragamuffin? How dare you—"

"Rest assured that Robin Hood has nothing but the most peaceable intentions," Mr. Agee cried.

Now the others were sitting up in bed, watching as Mr. Conroy staggered toward the child poised on the windowsill. There was no hint of shock or skepticism in his face, only a bitter yearning. "Me too," he whispered hoarsely. "Take me with you."

Mr. Agee's helpless glance fastened on Bloom, who smiled sadly, then shook his head.

Mr. Agee stared down at the old man. "It's too late, Leo. You'll have to stay with yourself."

Miss Cox marched toward the windowsill, fury in her face. As she reached out to the small figure crouching there, Mr. Agee turned and grabbed at a tree branch bobbing just beyond the opening. "Up and away!" he shouted.

Then, with a swoop, he disappeared into the night.

Bloom smiled. So did all the others, even Mr. Conroy.

All the others, that is, except Miss Cox.

She had fainted.

The sun was shining on Sunneyvale once again, shining on the front lawn where its residents had gathered.

From a truck in the driveway, several young men unloaded plants and rose bushes, planting them in place along the spaded borders on either sides.

Mr. Mute nodded approvingly to his companions. "We'll have the garden out in back," he said. "Let's put tomatoes along the fence and maybe some squash and those red poppies, the ones that open in the mornings."

He turned as Mrs. Dempsey crossed the lawn to the group, carrying a picnic basket. "I packed a lunch for us," she announced. "We can take a taxi to the lake." She glanced down toward the white cat prowling at her feet. "I've promised Mickey a look at that lake for years now."

Mrs. Weinstein smiled. "Let's ask Mr. Conroy. He can bring his grandchild. Kids love water."

From the open doorway of the entrance behind them a wailing voice arose: "Mr. Agee? Mr. Agee? Has anyone seen Mr. Agee?"

Mr. Weinstein shrugged. "I'll bet he's at the ball game!"

"Or the movies," Mrs. Weinstein said.

Mrs. Dempsey nodded. "Definitely at the movies. Probably one of those Kung-Fu pictures."

The old people laughed, their voices rising and clear in the afternoon sunlight.

Hearing them, Bloom nodded. Standing inside the men's dormitory he finished packing his tattered suitcase, then picked it up and carried it down the hall to the back exit. Moving into the yard, he saw Mr. Conroy playfully kicking the old tin can across the grass, too absorbed to notice as Bloom hurried past him into the alleyway beyond.

Only when Miss Cox's voice rose from within the residence did Mr. Conroy look up.

"Mr. Agee, Mr. Agee—where are you?"

Mr. Conroy smiled to himself. "Wherever he is, you won't find him."

Bloom turned and started down the alleyway unnoticed. The last thing he heard was the sound of Mr. Conroy at play, happily kicking the can.

Bloom walked down the street, suitcase in hand.

He'd been walking a long time, for the sun was

already setting, but now he reached his destination. Pausing beside an iron gate in a high stone wall, he peered through the bars at a wooden sign set before the sprawling structure beyond, reading the lettering—*Driftwood Convalescent Home*.

He opened the gate; it creaked behind him as he walked down the driveway to where a woman with a nurse's uniform stood waiting in the front doorway.

"Mr. Bloom?" she said.

He nodded.

"Good, we've been expecting you." She turned and entered, leading Bloom down the hall and into a large room at one side. Halting near the doorway, she nodded at Bloom, her voice rising through the somber silence. "Excuse me, ladies and gentlemen. Our new guest has arrived."

Bloom stared at a dreary roomful of old people seated in the shadows. As they looked up, he glanced past them, staring through the picture window beyond. Then he smiled and stepped forward.

Outside, twilight was falling. . . .

SHOCKINGLY FRIGHTENING!

Just *TRY* Not to Be Frightened!

__OUT ARE THE LIGHTS
by Richard Laymon   (B90-519, $2.75)
Every week there's a new episode of "Schreck." Every week a new victim faces horror while you watch. Who'd ever think movies made right here in our own town could be so authentic-looking? The blood looks so...bloody. The actors look so scared. And you'd swear all those horrible things are really happening. It's only a movie...or is it?

__THE KEEPSAKE
by Paul Huson   (B90-790, $2.95)
It was only a souvenir of Ireland—a small stone that bore, if you looked very closely, the suggestion of a human face. She couldn't know that only the power of St. Patrick had kept its evil in check through the centuries...that in her own home, when the lights were out, it could become a gateway for an unimaginable malevolence with a thirst for blood and for her unborn child.

_THE WOODS ARE DARK
by Richard Laymon   (F90-518, $2.75)
It was business as usual in Barlow until Johnny Robbins broke the rules and returned to the scene of The Trees to save the girl he couldn't resist. The Devil had his number now and wouldn't let him escape. But he ran anyway, taking the victims and pursued by the terror that stalked the woods.

GREAT SCIENCE FICTION
From WARNER...

___**ALIEN**
by Alan Dean Foster   (30-577, $3.25)
Astronauts encounter an awesome galactic horror on a distant planet.
But it is only when they take off again that the real horror begins. For the
alien is now within the ship, within the crew itself. And a classic
deathtrap suspense begins.

___**WHEN WORLDS COLLIDE**
by Philip Wylie and Edwin Balmer   (30-539, $2.75)
When the extinction of Earth is near, scientists build rocket ships to evac-
uate a chosen few to a new planet. But the secret leaks out and touches
off a savage struggle among the world's most powerful men for the
million-to-one chance of survival.

___**AFTER WORLDS COLLIDE**
by Philip Wylie and Edwin Balmer   (30-383, $2.75)
When the group of survivors from Earth landed on Bronson Beta, they
expected absolute desolation. But the Earth people found a breathtak-
ingly beautiful city encased in a huge metal bubble, filled with food for a
lifetime but with no trace either of life—or death. Then the humans
learned that they were not alone on Bronson Beta....

To order, use the coupon below. If you prefer to use your
own stationery, please include complete title as well as
book number and price. Allow 4 weeks for delivery.